THE OTHER SIDE OF THE RAINBOW

NIRANJAN NAYAK

INDIA • SINGAPORE • MALAYSIA

ISBN
Paperback 979-8-89556-968-9
Hardcase 979-8-89588-624-3

I dedicate this modest literary endeavour to my father, Late **Abhilash Chandra Nayak** and my mother Late **Shakuntala Nayak** for their lifelong struggles to make me what I am today.

DISCLAIMER

This is a work of fiction. Names, characters, places, and incidents are either the product of the author's imagination or used fictitiously.

Any resemblance to actual events or persons, living or dead, is entirely coincidental. The author makes no claims about the accuracy or authenticity of the information presented in this book. This book is not intended to be taken as a factual or historical account. The views and opinions expressed in this book are those of the characters and do not necessarily reflect the views of the author or publisher.

The author and publisher disclaim any liability for any damage or injury caused by the use of information contained in this book.

CONTENTS

Acknowledgement *7*

A Foreword *9*

A Prologue That's Not A Prologue *13*

PART-ONE

It Begins With Him 19

PART-TWO

I, Me And Myself 56

PART-THREE

He And Me: One Sky, Two Earths 81

PART-FOUR

Rummaging Through The Shadows
And Silhouettes 121

A Tree Sheds Its Last Leaf *209*

Epilogue: The Road To Redemption *231*

ACKNOWLEDGEMENT

Every work of art needs the presence of a catalyst to help the artist contemplate the completion of his art. I will fail in my duty if I don't acknowledge the inspirational role of some beautiful people, whose association with me has brought me closer to the fulfilment of my dream and a promise I made to myself years ago.

I will always remain grateful to my sister Namita Nayak for generating within me an ardent inclination towards literature. I will run out of words to express my obligation to my wife Sasmita for her intuitive input to give shape to my unbridled imagination. She has edited the manuscript with extraordinary patience and perseverance to ensure an error-free draft. I wish I could ever emulate a tiny fragment of that enviable dedication. My son Anurag has all along been a pillar of strength to me. Ironically, he has taken the role of my mentor at a time when I was grappling with my dwindling self-belief. I am grateful to a brilliant colleague of mine, Dr. Debasish Pati for taking the pain to go through the manuscript and suggest some quintessential structural changes. I thank all my friends for the enthusiasm they have shown to bring me closer to my goal. I thank Ravenshaw College, my Alma Mater for planting dreams in my eyes and for giving me the courage to fulfil some of them. Last but not least, I thank Notion Press for providing me with the necessary logistic support to ensure the publication of this book.

A FOREWORD

Debasisha Pati

If there's a book that you want to read, but it hasn't been written yet, then you must write it.

–Toni Morrison

A book is bigger than its author. It applies to all authors vis a vis their debut books. With *The Other Side of the Rainbow*, Niranjan Nayak, the poet and academic forays into fiction in his late fifties. It is something other than writerly ambition that seems to have propelled Nayak into producing this book. A private emotion arising out of a lived experience of Nayak's has, with the years, snowballed into a story so huge that it clamours, as it were, for a public appearance. And this magnificent first novel is the consequence of the clamour.

Is the novel a slice of life lived by the author? An unapologetic *yes*. How can it be otherwise? Art affects because the artist has been affected by what she sets out to represent through her art. In fiction, what is narrated is real; only how it is narrated is imaginary. The craft of the novelist consists in storying the real. Niranjan

Nayak has made the most of his craft in the friendship saga that *The Other Side of the Rainbow* is. The kind of authenticity that the incidents depicted in the novel exude reinforces the reader's belief that the novelist has either lived them or witnessed them from very close quarters. Therefore, in Nayak's novel, the book rather than the biography of the author hints at the autobiographical in it.

A college teacher of English literature for more than three decades, Nayak is exposed to a wide range of classic novels. In his novel, however, he, unlike many academic novelists, has refrained from tinkering with the rules of the game, both in the conception of the content and in its narration. His is largely a bildungsroman, a time-tested novelistic form couched in a linear narrative. As a storyteller, Nayak's core belief seems to be that it is the story that sells. Primarily focused on his subject, he has no linguistic pretensions. In a language that is crystalline, the novelist tells his story. A story that in turn sears and soothes.

In *The Other Side of the Rainbow*, Nayak portrays friendship, a subject that enjoys an eternal appeal of sorts for readers. What makes it a fresh friendship novel is the nuances carefully etched into the narrative. Far from being its glorification, the novel problematizes friendship. For instance, it is not about what a friend can do for another; it is about what one, despite being a well-meaning friend cannot do for another. Friendship is shown as both liberating and limiting. And so on. The novel hits upon the strange in the familiar. That Nayak achieves this feat without euphemizing or exaggerating only adds to the strength of his novel.

W. B. Yeats has famously written: "How can we know the dancer from the dance?" Thus, content and form are inextricable. Just as a river creates its own banks, so does content determine its form. Nayak has made a narratological experimentation in his novel by having two first-person narrators. Though technically a striking departure, it appears too natural to be even noticeable simply because the story demands it. As a tale of two friends to be told with honesty and without authorial intrusion, the novel requires twin first-person narrators for its effective telling. The counterbalancing of perspectives of the two friends in the novel gives its plot a strength, uniquely its own.

I wish I did not know the author, personally. Then `I would be more objective towards his work. This is what I thought when Niranjan Nayak shared the manuscript with me for my inputs, if any. When I finished reading the novel, I thanked God that I knew the author. I was surprised by how different the author I witnessed in the book was from the person I had known for a couple of decades. A merry-go-lucky guy sitting down to write a deeply moving account of pain and loss in the lives of people who are too young to lose. This was the closest I came to realizing that artists and the persons they are happen to be different entities.

Unputdownable, the book will haunt you. It does not promise the luxury of catharsis.

1. Debasisha Pati, PhD teaches literatures in English at Department of English and Modern European Languages, University of Allahabad, Prayagraj, India.

A PROLOGUE THAT'S NOT A PROLOGUE ...

You fail to see the invisible me

The tumult in a silent zone

I rob my heart with shiny paints

But darkness shrouds them all

You fail to see the invisible me

That was when it all began: a deep, unrelenting yearning to return to a past that had slipped from my grasp. It was a journey as treacherous as plunging into the depths of the ocean to retrieve the precious pearls of your youth, lost in a battle with the turbulent waves of life. And in that struggle for survival, you sacrificed your most cherished memories. "Initially, it might look like a rambling story with too many digressions. But I assure you, as you go further, you will find it difficult to dissociate yourself from the course of this narrative."

I pulled out the old trunk from under the bed of my son's room. The aluminium sheets have not lost their lustre even after thirty years. This was the suitcase that my father had purchased for me when I was getting ready to leave my home forever for higher studies. It was perhaps the most traumatic period of his life. The fear, insecurities and uncertainties associated with my obstinate decision to study in a college far away from my home, gave my father a few sleepless nights. Finally, he took the toughest decision of his life: allowing me to make my destiny when the chances of breaking it were always very high. My father left everything to the mercy of the almighty God, who, he could trust, only when the situation warranted it that way.

My father purchased a strong and big suitcase for his pale, frail, and ailing son, though he had serious doubts about how long he would survive in that hostile terrain called college hostel, with odds weighing heavy against me due to the erratic intervention of my truant destiny. But he couldn't afford to disappoint his only son after his reasonable success in the secondary school board examination when the latter was too excited to study outside, in the college of his dreams.

I pulled the trunk with a lot of effort, flexing my waning body muscles. The old lock hung from the hook with its characteristic tenacity. My wife was fast asleep in our bedroom. The outdoor unit of the old Air

Conditioner was drumming with an ominous sound and fury. I took advantage of the sound resonating in our bedroom, making it almost impossible for any other sound to intrude inside. My wife was used to this sound. With a lightweight small hammer, I tried to break open the old and heavily rusted lock. After six to seven merciless strokes, the lock gave up its resistance to guard my privacy, a job that it had been doing with unwavering commitment for the last thirty years. I opened the trunk. On one side, there were a few old clothes. At the centre of the trunk, there were some old books of my college days with a thick layer of dust on them, that could penetrate through the narrow gaps of the manually aligned aluminium casket. The remaining portion contained a small number of greeting cards, an old album and nearly a dozen letters from my father and my long-lost friends.

I flipped through the pages of the album in a hurry. On the first page was a postcard-size photo of my parents, the only one they had, before my father's retirement. In photographs, my father always looked younger than my mother. After giving birth to four children, my mother braced a premature old age. There were three photos of my three sisters. They all looked young, pretty and contented, though contentment always stayed away from our family for one reason or another. There were also some photos of my friends, both from my school and college. Then I saw one old postcard-size black and white photograph, clicked in an old-fashioned manual camera and a passport-size photograph of a young girl around eighteen years old. In the first photo, the photographer captured images of four youngsters posing before the camera while standing on the sprawling golden sands of Puri sea beach. He had not failed to catch the excitement of four half-naked boys, ready to jump into the sea. It was a shot taken by a professional photographer. The photo looked hazy and the faces were blurred with white smudges here and there. But there was one smiling face in the photograph, that had withstood the ravages of time. He stood there in the centre with his left hand tossed on my shoulder. This was the face I was looking for so desperately. I got it almost after an era.

The passport-size photo belonged to one of my classmates, with whom I had always shared a warm relationship, till we parted ways after a misunderstanding. But much before that, she had given me the photo with a request to get it attested by a gazetted officer, and forgetting all ethics, I kept it secretly in my wallet with no good intention of ever returning it to her. For some strange reason, she had never asked for her photograph. She might have forgotten it, or she might have wanted me to keep it with me forever. I held both the photos in my hand with a nostalgic remembrance, sweet yet sad. The longing to go back to the past with a time machine, as I have seen in movies, was so irrepressible. This could be the beginning of an untold story, that promises no end. Past doesn't haunt us in a linear pattern. It visits us often, either with all its alluring familiarity in our dreams or in the form of a nightmare to rob at least one instalment of our peaceful sleep.

PART-ONE

IT BEGINS WITH HIM

THE DEVIL AND THE DEEP SEA

The beginning of an end, the end of a beginning, and this is the endless cycle. Is life all about musing, brooding, being happy and not being happy, musing and not musing, brooding and not brooding, living and dying? Life is like that and not like that. Life, as I interpret it, is a questionable conviction, a journey through a deep, dense forest, dark and mysterious, and very truly "a tale told by an idiot full of sound and furies, signifying nothing". Life is like this, like that, not like this, not like that. Life is a paradox.

I lost a battle yesterday, the one I had been fighting for years, the one that could have defined the 'me' within myself, my quest for my identity that was playing hide and seek with me ever since the day I was born. I lost a part of myself, a part I can never retrieve. One more lesson from life: life is all about those millions of losses and lies that someone like me has been compelled to accept with a mixed sense of rebellion and resignation. Life teaches us to accept, what it holds in its kitty for us. Life is just a manifestation of the invisible destiny. I am not the only one who has lost a battle. There are millions like me and they are all labelled as losers. "A man's destination is not his destiny", a great man had once said. The reverse may be equally true to someone like me.

It was a normal morning the day after, bright and sunny. The flowers glowed with colourful radiance. The sky was happy, the birds were happy and the earth had no reason to be unhappy. None of them knew I had lost a battle yesterday; the most decisive battle of my life. How does it actually matter? I am just a dark speck in this universe, and my tiny existence ends before it begins to assume some significance and shape. I am just a nobody trying to be somebody or a delusional somebody, who has been a nobody all along.

We all live with a sense of foreboding that clings to us as long as we are alive. We know about our fears, our hallucinations, our delusions. We accept their inevitability as our unfailing shadow. In a long sojourn to get back that precious part of ourselves, we have lost somewhere on the road, in a forest, in the river or in the sea, the quintessential part that we know, we might find hard to retrieve. But still, we don't give up. We move on, carrying the burden of our false hope on our tired heads. We never give up, though we know giving up can solve our existential crisis. Giving up is the only elusive elixir that can rejuvenate our tired souls.

I saw the devil in my dream. People boast of having a glimpse of the God in heaven in their dreams. Not that I don't believe in God, but the devil always fascinates me. I had once invoked his unholy spirit to be my patron. The devil has his sense of dignity, which he upholds with rigid stubbornness, which God doesn't have. God is flexible in His own way, whereas the devil is committed and more tenacious than his lenient counterpart. That was why I wanted him as my master: shrewd, audacious, pretentious, malevolent and gritty. My heart became the battleground, where the devil was fighting his most relentless battle against God, forcing me every day to defer the finality, that could have changed the course of my life, a not-so-ordinary life of an ordinary person. But how long?

THE GENESIS

My parents were poor. We were four siblings: Pari Didi, Sony Didi, Babu Bhai and me, the youngest, Arun. I distinctly remember my mother going to bed on an empty stomach, convincing her gullible children with one story or another at least twice a week. I had seen poverty with all its ugliness from a very close quarter. We lived in a single room, with a partially damaged thatched roof. At night, we were very few among all the impoverished families in my village to view a part of the silvery moon through the weather-beaten thatched roof. On rainy days, our mother used to struggle to find a dry floor in a room, soaked with rainwater where her children could sleep. But we never used to mind that, as much to our delight, rainwater intruded into our home through the moth-eaten threshold. It was fun for us to see water accumulating on the damp earth and gradually forming a puddle on the floor, where we were used to sleeping in a huddle. Sleep deprivation was never a concern for us. We used to go out and float paper boats on rainwater with other children of our age during the day. If it rained at night, my mother had to keep herself busy keeping earthen pots on the floor to collect the rainwater dripping through the multiple leakages on the cover overhead; that was just an apology for a roof. The moth-eaten threshold was secured by recycled cotton sacks to prevent the inflow of water. We were four malnourished children with protruding bellies. Poverty had planted its stubborn foot in my house. Frequent fights between my parents were a common ugly spectacle for us. But we didn't know the profoundly unpalatable truth that domestic bickering is the only viable option for poor couples before they get ready to sleep on an empty stomach. They fight, reconcile and love in their desperate attempts to compromise with their misfortune.

I was reading in a village government school, whereas my siblings were not so lucky to be enrolled. They had to run small errands to help my father earn whatever little he could from selling fritters and fried peanuts. My mother cooked them in a makeshift oven in our backyard and packed them hot in a bamboo basket for my father to carry on his head to the nearest school, where unfortunately, I was studying and then to the nearest local market, after the usual school hours. He had learnt a funny song from my grandfather and was singing it in his nasalised voice to attract customers. As a child, I disliked the song as much as I disliked my father. My schoolmates sometimes teased me, calling me the son of a pakodawala. I had never heard anyone showing any appreciation for his weird song or his mannerisms. He was just poor and pitiable, an archetypal character, fighting a battle with his unkind destiny for our survival. Never in his life, had he been treated either with love or sympathy, by his children, who could never forgive him for making their life so difficult due to his incompetence. But he was my father, my mother's husband, the head of our family. We all owe, whatever identity we have, to him.

THE PROPHECY?

Since my childhood, I had been a promising student, at least, that was what, my teachers always believed. There were some fifteen to twenty students in my class. The school was run in a temporary structure with a roof made of zinc sheets to protect us from sun and rain. We had to sit on the earthen floor, spreading a mat made from palm leaf in the absence of proper sitting arrangement. An old bespectacled man, with a frail frame and shrunken cheekbone, was teaching us mathematics, science, social studies and our mother tongue. Studying the English language before class four was strictly forbidden. For four years, we all got used to listening to our omniscient narrator, without having the freedom of interrupting him. The fear of being spanked on our butts mercilessly by a long cane, prevented us from asking any questions or correcting him, even when we knew he was wrong. All of us had more fear than respect for him. On his wizened face, sorrow and anxiety had left their indelible impressions. He was just one among us, living with a greater sense of deprivation than his poor, malnourished, half-starved students.

His occasional anger was just a manifestation of the mental turmoil he was going through, in his attempts to provide a reasonably decent life to his wife and children.

The common perception of all villagers was that he was more privileged than most of them, because of his government job. But this common perception was always based on some fundamentally flawed premises, 'because, limited privileges become the root cause of unlimited expectations, which are hard to fulfil'. The poor, illiterate villagers were perhaps oblivious to the fact that, he had a bigger family with much bigger expectations to fulfil with a meagre salary.

However, he was very fond of me. I was perhaps the only student who could sit on his lap and read out the multiplication chart loudly to my jealous classmates, and I gloated over that feeling of self-importance. I was simply a part of his fragmented aspiration, the lone bright spot in his hopeless life. One day, he told one of the parents after the publication of my annual result, "You know, Arun will one day be an officer. He is just outstanding. If I live that long, then, that will be the happiest day of my life." A village school teacher lives his life in anonymity, always underrated and ignored. Once in a blue moon, a student of my calibre brings a ray of hope in his uneventful life".

Clouds rumbled on the distant horizon and the teacher had to cut his bragging short. He had to rush home before it started raining. Dhani Sir (my village school teacher) didn't have the sixth sense to understand what clouds said.

THE DISASTER AND THE AFTERMATH

My father died when I was a student in class three. His death was abrupt and unexpected like someone being struck by lightning while walking on the road. I was too young to understand what death exactly meant to my family. I saw everyone crying and started crying too without trying to know, why they were crying. Later on, my brother told me that, he died of cardiac arrest. But poor people rarely have heart attacks, because their starved arteries are never blocked. That was what I learnt much later as a college student. My mother didn't have enough money to perform the last rites of my father. The condolences of our near and dear ones meant nothing to the impoverished household, mourning the death of the lone breadwinner of the family. My mother sat dumb in one corner, staring at the infinite darkness enveloping her. Her eyes looked pallid like those of a dead fish. I could neither comprehend the reason behind her stupefied sorrow nor the panic that seized my brother and sisters. Dhani Sir was standing under the nearby mango tree, watching me with pain and concern in his eyes. When my relatives carried the body of my father for cremation, headed by my elder brother, who was holding a sheaf of burning straw, and an iron chopper, Dhani Sir came to me and hugged me tight with tearful eyes. I didn't know, why I reciprocated with an inconsolable sob.

Perhaps, for the first time in my life, I realised something was terribly wrong with my family.

After the cremation, my relatives returned. My uncle served them flattened rice, curd, and jaggery. My elder brother was standing there, half-petrified with fear and concern. Unlike others, I could not find any trace of tears in his eyes. There was a strange cynicism, a cruel defiance, a loss of faith in providence, reflected on his pale face. Perhaps he was gathering the courage to face the uncertainties, lying ahead. He knew the magnitude of this disaster and how that could affect him, his dreams and aspirations if he had any. He knew he would soon dive into a turbulent whirlpool and rising out of it could be almost impossible. He was getting ready for the greatest sacrifice he had to make in his life with calmness and fortitude. Later in my life, when I started reading Greek Tragedies, I kept wondering, why Aristotle was so selective about tragic heroes. Why can't a common man be the hero of a Tragedy? Perhaps, Aristotle was twice biased in his views on tragic heroes.

We spent the remaining eleven days, mourning the death of the head of the family, my father, who was managing this poor household comprising of six members, including himself, was working hard day and night to cater to our bare minimum needs. But somehow everyone close to us knew that, the mourning was overshadowed by an overwhelming sense of insecurity, that was getting bigger and bigger every day. None of my family members knew, what the next day would bring for them. We observed every funeral rite with profound austerity, like eating once a day, sleeping on the damp earthen floor and keeping an earthen lamp alight day and night. Deep within her heart, my mother had a temporary sense of relief, because we didn't have enough rice at home to cook twice daily. By keeping ourselves half-starved, we could pay our sincere homage to our father who departed early, leaving his family in a state of utter despair. The fear within my mother was growing with a baleful intensity: the fear of not being able to feed her children, the fear of not being able to protect them and make them stand on their feet.

My brother sat under the mango tree, his eyes fixed on the crumbling hut that we called our home. His thoughts were running faster than a wounded animal, chased by a predatory beast. I was in a state of mystification about the bizarre behaviour of the elders in the family. It was not that, I was not missing my father; but the absence of someone could be such a terrible experience, I didn't have any idea. The pall of gloom was growing like darkness on a moonless night in my household. I didn't appreciate the wailing of our visiting relatives, their brazen demonstration of sorrow, their apprehension of the inevitability of the catastrophe that was on its way to hit us hard with all its ugliness and cruelty. But after they left, I was feeling sad and lonely. I was clueless about what exactly was happening around me. My confusion kept growing with each passing day. Ironically, my maternal uncle, who never used to visit our house due to some serious misunderstanding with my mother, came once with my aunt to offer his condolences, and before his departure, he gave a sly hint about something to my mother. My mother flared up and asked him to leave immediately and never to come there again. Her sudden outburst didn't come as a surprise to any of us. We had heard from my mother how selfishly he had thrown my aged and ailing grandfather out of his house a few days after his marriage. After he left, I heard my mother speaking to herself: "I would rather give poison to my children". She kept repeating the sentence as if she was expecting some kind of endorsement from us. But we were too naïve to react.

THE PURPLE SKY

My mother mortgaged the lone piece of cultivable land my father owned through inheritance, to perform his funeral rites. On the eleventh day, we were practically purged of the impurity caused due to my father's death. My mother and my elder brother had invited ten Brahmins to decontaminate us with their blessings. All of them had one thing in common; being ostensibly and shamelessly gluttonous and greedy. However, they were not so miserly while bestowing their blessings upon a crestfallen family and I would always remember them with a sense of gratitude. Later in my life, many who became my friends were Brahmins. They were decent people, educated, cultured and civilised. It's poverty and deprivation, that at times, bring the worst out of us. Those, who had come to our home on the eleventh day, were invariably poor and marginalised. The nobility of their caste did not help them access any privilege. So, most of them remained greedy, gluttonous and manipulative. One may blame it on their circumstantial compulsions.

I was happy because my mother gave me a brand new shirt and a half pant, purchased from the weekly local market in our village. Everyone in our family, including our near relatives, was also given new clothes to wear. With shaved heads and clean white dresses, my brother and I looked like small, cute, benign ghosts. But the irony was, we were more dead than alive and we did not know that. My mother was wearing a plain white saree. One of my aunts told me, she would never be able to wear anything colourful. On the eleventh day, I noticed her bare wrist: someone had removed all the glass bangles she was wearing with so much love and adulation: the pride of every married woman, the tingling testimony of the completeness of her marital status, the pride of being with her man to lead her, walk beside her, hold her hand and give her a sense of fulfilment. Someone had wiped the tiny speck of vermillion off from her head. Draped in a white saree, my mother loitered from one end of the house to another. I was watching her from a distance, watching her pale face, her emaciated frame, the unkempt hair on her head and the beads of perspiration on her forehead. Everything looked so cruel and bizarre; I clutched my mother's hand and cried. She held me tight in her thin, bony hands, her fingers almost hurt me. But she did not let me go. She was in a trance, a transcendental state when the soul wishes to leave the mundane pain and suffering on the ground and soar high up in search of peace, but the wishful escape never materialises as the soul remains in a state of suspension between the desire to die and the compulsion to live to keep others, one feels accountable to, alive.

I looked at the purple sky. I was looking for my father in the clouds, painted by the setting sun. I found a small cloudlet, that vaguely resembled my father. It gradually got bigger and diffused in the monstrous enormity of the evening sky. I lost my father before I could trace him. I lost my father among the clouds and in the darkness. But what I didn't know was, that I would never be able to get him back for my sad and lonely mother, for my nervous brother, and for my insecure sisters.

We look for a trace of life, trapped within the rubble after the disaster. That is what every human being essentially is; incurably optimistic yet invariably scared of the inevitable. My mother and my elder brother were getting ready to start from the beginning. The relics of what we had yesterday, were painfully disturbing. For my brother, it was too difficult a task to handle. Neither did he have the strength, nor the maturity, to give some kind of shape to our fragmented world. He had no one to fall back upon, no hand to hold and no beam of light to follow. He was fighting for a lost cause and he knew, he would succumb to the onslaught of a malevolent destiny. Life taught him the hardest lesson when he was least prepared for it.

A few weeks after my father's death, we were grappling with hunger and poverty and the possibility of getting any help from any friend or relative to overcome the worst-ever existential crisis, seemed very bleak then. Though young, I could still sense the despondency of my mother, the desperation of my brother, and the helplessness of the other two younger siblings. With my tiny head, all I could understand was that my family was in deep trouble and there was no quick fix, no shortcut to find a remedy for our sustenance.

Dhani Sir came one day to meet my mother. He had brought a few candies for me from the nearby variety store. He took my mother to one corner and spoke to her in a suppressed voice. No pleasant thing is ever discussed in a low voice, that no one can hear except the person for whom it is meant. I was watching my mother curiously from a distance. I saw her shaking her head vigorously, an unmistakable sign of refusal which was not even difficult for a small kid like me to understand. Then the suppressed consultation gradually got louder and louder and took the shape of an animated conversation. Perhaps Dhani Sir was not happy with my mother, perhaps his proposal was not acceptable to her, perhaps my mother had treated my favourite teacher with some disrespect; something I had never seen her doing ever in her life. She was so shy, docile and meek like many village women, living with their stupefied silence in a patriarchal setup in their family. I stood perplexed, watching both of them, discussing something with so much seriousness tempered with unhappiness. I was always fond of Dhani Sir for publicly pampering me in the classroom, but no son could ever be happy, if an outsider treated his mother, even with the mildest kind of harshness. I was angry with him. I wanted to throw away the candies he had given me a while ago and throw up the one, revolting inside my tummy. Dhani Sir, no matter how powerful a person he could be, or how much affection he had shown me, didn't have any right to speak to my mother in a raised voice.

The agitated conversation came to an abrupt end and Dhani Sir spun to his heel, the signs of disappointment and anger written large on his face. The last sentence that he spoke and I could hear was, "Then send him to the brick kiln, he will earn enough to feed you". Dhani Sir left our place, disappointed and angry. My mother was standing like a weatherbeaten idol of a partially demolished temple, with her eyes fixed on Dhani Sir as he was storming out of our house. She wiped her tears with one end of her saree and looked in the direction where I was standing. I ran to my mother and hugged her. Both of us clung to each other, her fingers caressing the ruffled hair on my head and my hands holding her in a tight embrace. For a while, I had a strange desire to get into her womb and stay there forever, far beyond the reach of my unsympathetic relatives and over-sympathetic Dhani Sir.

My mother was sobbing. The sound coming from her throat was scary. Was she crying or was she cursing her fate or all those deities she used to worship with ardent devotion and austerity? I couldn't decipher. I simply wanted to hold her tightly and make her forget all our agonies. I wanted to be the fire to melt her frozen sorrows.

RAIN AND HOPE

It rained throughout last night. I could see flashes of lightning through the gaps of the half-broken wooden window of the room we used for sleeping at night. In no way did it fit the contemporary version of a bedroom. It was all we had besides an extended terrace, where my mother used to cook for us. Rainwater was dripping through the thin patches of straw used by my father to cover the roof overhead. My mother was busy putting clay pots to prevent the room from getting wet with rainwater. She was unusually calm that night.

In the morning, I saw her shouting at my uncle, my father's younger brother, who was perceptibly angry with my mother for reasons best known to him. He left our place in a hurry, carrying the anger in his heart that his conscience didn't allow him to use on his brother's widow. After he left, my mother sat in a corner and wept nearly for an hour. Her eyes were swollen and her face was flushed. She moved restlessly in the courtyard, mumbling something in an inaudible voice. My brother and sisters were watching her from a distance, their eyes betraying their helplessness and insecurity. For the first time perhaps, she forgot to cook our mid-day meal. She banged her head against the wall, when I said, "Maa, I am hungry". She was cursing herself, her irreversible destiny, quietly in the quietness of a hot and humid July afternoon.

I was trying to get some sleep. But seeing my brothers and sister wide awake, I realised that it was not a usual rainy night. The rain, the booming thunder, and the eerie silence prevailing inside made the night unusually ominous. "The worst is yet to come, but it will come, hit us hard and leave no scope for us, save an abject and unconditional surrender to the malicious designs of our omnipotent destiny".

It was an incessant downpour. The clay pots put below the patchy leakages on our weather-battered roof were getting full with rainwater, threatening to spill out of the pots. My mother was looking for the old aluminium containers to put over the brimming clay pots. We had never seen so much rain in our life. The rain kept pattering upon the roof, the trees, and the spread-out tin sheets kept by someone near our house. Perhaps the sky was crying like my mother. But my mother's sorrows were too condensed to dissolve into a downpour. I was sure, one day there would be a cloud burst, a deluge to sweep away the remnants of the hope within us.

We spent nearly a sleepless night and just before the outbreak of the dawn, we dozed off for a while. The rain subsided. The twittering of the birds woke us up. There was sunlight outside and the leaves of the trees looked wet but resplendent. There were multiple puddles around our house. Some of my neighbours were busy with their fishing nets. I thought of my father: how he used to carry the net to the poolside while going out for a bath. For a while, I missed him. Babu Bhai had never caught fish with a fishing net. But seeing the disappointment in my eyes, he dismantled the net from the old bamboo ceiling and slowly walked towards the pool.

My mother was cooking rice in the clay pot on our veranda. Sitting nearby, I could inhale the smell of freshly cooked rice. The rice was boiling inside the pot as my mother stirred the stuff with a wooden ladle. Something was boiling within her too. The ugly spat with my uncle, her throwing the tantrum at Dhani Sir, the future uncertainties, the disproportionate burden on the shoulder of Babu Bhai, the shapeless days ahead, that could get uglier than she could expect and much more. She was lost in her thoughts while stirring the boiling rice absent-mindedly.

I was waiting for my brother to come with his catch for the day. The sun was slowly climbing up the sky, diffusing the cluster of clouds with an arrogant defiance. Was there hope in the sky? I wasn't sure. I was just waiting for my brother to come back. I was preoccupied with the prospect of slurping down the fish curry from the bowl.

THE UNSUNG MENTOR

One evening, a few days after my father's death, Dhani Sir paid a second visit to our house on his old bicycle. I was navigating a discarded bicycle tyre with a bamboo stick in my hand, through the narrow dusty village street. The tired sun was getting ready to go down the horizon after blazing down upon the earth for ten long hours. The sky was draped in a mellow orange glow. Dhani Sir waved at me, and I raised my hands to bow to him without any enthusiasm; it was just a perfunctory gesture. I was too busy with all those intricate manoeuvres to run the tyre through the numerous interminable bends on the road, that leads to my home.

Dhani Sir got off his bicycle and kicked its rear stand hard to keep it stable and erect. He slowly walked towards the entrance of my house. My mother was sitting in the courtyard, her eyes fixed on the empty evening sky. When she saw him, she stood up, pulling the veil of her white saree to cover her sad face partially. She spread a straw mat on the floor and asked sir to sit there. Sir talked to my mother for approximately an hour. But that day my mother neither looked angry nor agitated. There was just a glint of concern mixed with fear in her eyes.

I had never seen Dhani Sir looking so happy at the school. There was a huge sense of relief on his face, which he was struggling to hide beneath his usual serious exterior. My mother got some tea for Sir. He sat there, sipping the steaming tea silently. Neither he nor my mother spoke to each other when Sir was sipping tea.

Dhani Sir got up and spoke to my mother, raising his voice with a newfound conviction, "From today onwards, he is my responsibility. You stop worrying about him. He will one day save you from the mess you are in. Just trust me and do never listen to any rumour, no matter how credible they sound." My mother simply nodded her head. He called me, placed his hand on my head and then rode his bicycle. Sir turned into a dark silhouette and slowly disappeared into the darkness before my eyes could follow him.

That night, while we were lying on our bed at night, my mother asked me, "Don't you miss your school these days?" "Yes", I said. I miss going to school, I miss my friends". From next Monday, you will go to school once again". Said my mother. I was happy for a while, but then I became sad. I had been enjoying unlimited freedom since the day my father died, no work and all play. No one had asked me to start going to school. Everyone in the family was busy, putting on whatever extra effort they could, to restore some kind of stability to our family. In their list of priorities, I didn't figure anywhere.

My mother stroked my tangled, greasy hair with her fingers, as I cuddled up to her. Then she spoke softly, "Dhani Sir told me today that, one day, you would become a babu and clear the mess we are in. Sir told me that you are a very bright boy and if properly guided, you may do well in the future. You are the only hope I have now. Babu bhai is already stressed. So, we all want you to study. But there is a small problem". "Problem"? I looked at my mother like a helpless lamb with a million questions in my eyes. "Yes, this time you have to stay in the hostel. You will visit home every Sunday. I know it will be tough for you to stay in a hostel in our absence. But trust me, you will gradually learn to enjoy that life."

Perhaps, that was what my mother was tutored in an hour-long training session by Dhani Sir: to speak to me, convince me and finally, with a bit of cajoling and blackmailing, make me agree to stay away from my family in a hostel and she did a good job. My grip on her arm slackened as a certain panic set in. Staying away from my mother was a bolt from the blue. I started sobbing holding my mother's hand, begging and pleading not to let me stay in the hostel. But my mother's body was stiff and cold. She was stroking my hair, but that seemed like a loveless gesture. She finally spoke, "We will all perish here; you, me, Babu Bhai, Pari, Sonu, all of us. We will die of starvation. I want you to live for us, to be the saviour of this family. Only you can do this. Dhani Sir believes in you. You are the youngest and the dearest in the family. Stay alive, at least, for me". My mother was crying while speaking to me. There was a shocking frankness in her voice, that sent a shiver down my spine. Perhaps her candid confession was the only tool in her bag to motivate me to stay in a hostel, run by the government. I later learnt it was not an ordinary hostel. It was a shelter home for orphans like me.

TO WALK ALONE THE DARK CORRIDOR

It's always scary for a child to be separated from his family. No child loves to sleep alone. No child loves to sleep in a room full of strangers. The most peaceful and secure place for a child is his mother's lap. My family was preparing me for the inevitable distress in my life. During the first few days, I was forced to sleep with my sister a few feet away from my mother. The next step was more difficult when my mother spread a straw mat in one corner of the room and asked me to sleep there. I could neither hold her hand nor get the smell of her body. Night after night, I had one nightmare: that of being pulled into darkness by a monster, though I had never seen one in my life. They just exist in the imagination of every child and spoil their peaceful sleep with a series of scary intrusions.

I was not exactly scared of darkness because, in a village in the absence of electricity, every child gets used to darkness. At night, my mother used to light up a kerosene lamp made out of an old tin can with a brass valve of a bicycle tube fitted on its lid, through which my mother inserted a rolled cotton wick. She poured some kerosene into the can with a dirty plastic funnel and tightened the lid. Then she struck a matchstick to light the lamp. The lamp kept flickering throughout the night, filling up the small room with light and patches of darkness that created the illusion of dark paintings of demons and witches on our mud walls. We had never used a hurricane lamp. Only a few families in our village, who were economically better off than many of us, had the luxury of using hurricane lamps.

I was just seven years old and the very idea of being away from my family sucked the life out of me. I was counting my days with an unending sense of trepidation. Once away from home, the monster would come and drag me away to a deep dark cavern, where he would tear me apart with his canine teeth and sharp claws.

I couldn't sleep at night and lost my appetite during the day. The premonition of something terrible happening to me once I was taken away from the comfort zone of my home made my life miserable. My mother could gauge the impact of the tempest blowing away the peace within me, my sense of security, and the stability that every child needs. But she was helpless. She could hear the faint bleating of the innocent lamb before it was led to the sacrificial altar. But it was her offering, her decision to learn to live without a part of her heart. She was getting ready to live and die, die and live with a deep chasm in her heart every minute, every second. The bond between my mother and me was getting weaker day by day. I, the silent sufferer, the clueless victim struggling with conflicting emotions, gradually distanced myself from my mother, from my family, from a bleak, dilapidated structure we were made to accept as our home.

LIFE ELSEWHERE

Life in a shelter home for the homeless was not easy. There were rows of grey, cheerless rooms with asbestos roofs, accommodating more than one hundred ill-fated children like me. Some had even more poignant pasts. We were allowed to sleep on the floor, ten of us in one room. Accepting a stranger as a friend was difficult. Building an acquaintance with an unknown face was more difficult. But in a place like this, one has to live with a few unhappy but curious faces, sad smiles, hostile grins and wait for the day when someone would stretch a friendly hand, share some happy and unhappy moments and let one feel that they belong to one common world: the world of the afflicted, a world that holds very little promises, a world that is no less claustrophobic than a dark labyrinthine passage that leads to infinite uncertainties.

There were a few big boys who were bullies and derived sadistic pleasure from our fear and suffering. They used to visit our rooms in the stillness of the night and wake us up to do things that kept us all traumatised. I, being the youngest and the newest, had to go through the worst in the form of physical and mental torture. After one week, I had the taste of the bitterness of being bullied, tortured, subjugated, physically and mentally defiled which threatened to continue forever. But the cliched statement: 'the darkest cloud has a silver lining', has some truth in it. Our suffering helped us to cling to one another, forge a common bond, and devise group strategies to thwart such attempts by our torturers. Our common afflictions brought us closer to one another. It helped us build up our resilience, our adaptability, and our newfound comradery. It helped us realise that there might be light at the end of the tunnel. At night, we, the ten little children started having lesser numbers of nightmares, punctuated by one or two dreams every now and then.

My mother used to come to visit me frequently. But gradually I could sense the glint of jealousy in the eyes of my not-so-lucky inmates. It would be better for me not to allow such occasional visits by someone who could desert her seven-year-old kid. One day, gathering all my courage, I told my mother not to come so frequently. Her reaction was palpable. Her face turned white like a sheet of paper. She handed over a packet containing homemade laddoos and walked slowly out of the campus. I came back to my room, holding back the tears in my eyes.

When my friends were enjoying the ladoos, relishing every bite, I was sitting on my mat, contemplating the most complex question one could ever ask oneself: "Do I still love my mother after all that she has done to me?" I didn't have the answer, and I could never know whether I was right or wrong that day.

I started going to school. Some of my schoolmates were happy to see me back, and others were not. The few hours I was spending at school were the happiest hours of my life. My teachers started treating me with more sympathy than love. But I was used to it. I studied with more seriousness and perseverance. Once again, I topped the term examination. It was more like the midfield exploits of a batsman who came back and scored a century after he retired hurt in the middle of the innings. Dhani Sir was the happiest man that day. He hugged me and whispered in my years, "The sky is not the limit for you". For a small child, the statement was highly philosophical. But all I could understand was that Dhani Sir was happy with my performance. On that day, with my half-matured mind, I decided to make him feel proud of me one day, no matter how hard I had to try for that. He was the man who didn't desert me at a time when all I needed was a saviour.

In class five, I got a government scholarship. It was a phenomenal achievement for a boy, staying in an orphanage. Dhani Sir came rushing to the hostel to break the news to me. His face was beaming like the morning sun. My mother also came in the afternoon. I was surprised to see my maternal uncle, who had come with my mother to congratulate me. My mother held my hand and cried. Was it the low-pressure-induced monsoon rain or an unseasonal cloudburst on the hinterland? I had no answer. But her tears dissolved the long-accumulated anger within me that had formed a painful lump somewhere in my heart. Before they all left, my uncle told me in an emphatic voice, "My boy, you will spend the upcoming Puja Holidays at our place". Was it an invite, a request or an order? I was too young to interpret. But I was certainly not amused, and what made me feel irritated was the stony silence of my mother on whose eyes I couldn't find any sign of approval or disapproval. I spent a sleepless night pondering over the sudden change in the equation of my mother's relationship with my uncle. How could she forgive him so easily? Why did my uncle ask me to spend the vacation at his place? I couldn't get a satisfactory answer to any of these questions. Finally, I gave up and closed my eyes to get some sleep.

The Block Development Officer visited our orphanage to felicitate me. The supervisor and the matron spared no chance to give a fabricated account of how loving and caring both of them were to me. When the B.D.O. looked at me for confirmation, I nodded my head. Then he told me that he would get me admitted to a good government school in the town where I would get better facilities. I was happy and sad at the same time. I would have been happier, had all those nine children staying with me got the same privilege. I was not exactly an idealist. But staying away from those children, who had shared the most difficult phase of my life, was certainly a difficult proposition. But I needed an escape route and I deserved one. I was duty bound to fulfil the lofty aspiration of Dhani Sir, my mentor, who had never expected, nor would ever expect anything from me except the psychological satisfaction of rescuing a poor helpless child from the gutter.

That night, when all those unhappy children with whom I had shared my own miseries were fast asleep, I was wide awake, thinking about the days ahead. I could foresee a road lying ahead of me, an unknown road leading to a better destination. I was getting mentally ready to tread on the unknown road, leaving a not-so-happy past far behind. But who could I share my sorrows with? The future looked hazy, uncertain, and deeply perplexing. I left the place with so many unshared guilt and shame and unsaid words, carrying a baggage of bitterness and fear on my shoulders.

THE BRIGHT SUNLIGHT

A new destination, new ambience, new friends, new dreams; my life was overhauled within two nights. Bidding farewell to my friends was difficult. They all came near the gate as I was waiting for a cycle rickshaw holding an old, rusted zinc suitcase. Dhani Sir was standing there, holding my hands, sweating profusely with nervousness. I can't exactly recall how I was feeling. It was a blend of varied emotions, cooking up in a cauldron. I was getting ready for a resurrection that demanded a determined obliteration of a painful past.

I mounted on the cycle rickshaw, holding one hand of Dhani Sir for support and waved at my friends. I didn't want to look back; perhaps I didn't have the courage. I was too young to understand the surge of emotions within me. But all I knew was that there was an uneasy feeling deep within me, a vacant space in my juvenile heart. The rickshaw puller dragged the rickshaw with a bit of difficulty. But slowly all three wheels started rolling on the uneven gravel path. One chapter of my life was closed and a new one was about to begin.

We got down from the rickshaw in front of a formidable looking iron gate with a majestic iron signboard on its top, bearing the name of the high school. The school established in 1944, some three years before India achieved independence, was christened after the then-king Maharaj Badrinarayan Rao. The campus was large enough to accommodate half of my village. There were a few concrete buildings, ringed by two large rows of asbestos rooms which were used as classrooms. The school was imparting teaching to students from class six to class eleven. Two boys' hostels were on the backside of the school, overlooking the sprawling bank of river Baitarani.

Dhani Sir, took me to hostel number 2, holding my hand all the way. We went to the office of the hostel warden who patted my back gently and called a peon to take my belongings to room no 5. For the first time in my life, I had the experience of sleeping on a wooden cot with a 100-watt electric bulb glowing overhead. There were five beds, four of which were arranged in two vertical columns, and one bed was horizontally placed near the wall, close to the only window the room had. The bed was used by a senior student from class vii. I was allotted a bed near the entrance.

The head boy came to meet me in the evening. He was a few inches taller than me and was wearing a stern expression on his face. He explained to me the rules and regulations of the hostel, the need to maintain discipline without fail, attend evening and morning prayers, show respect to the seniors, and take lunch and dinner during routine hours. I listened to him quietly, nodding my head in agreement. He didn't know my past. It was difficult for him to understand that, what he considered painful was nothing short of a luxury for me. He was in a state of mystification when he didn't find any visible disappointment on my face.

I spent my first night in a state of animation, tossing now and then on my new bed. For a while, I was feeling a bit jittery with the thought of what would happen to me in case I fell from the bed while asleep. How bad the injury would be? Whether the hostel had some rogue elements who would bully me at night and make me do those disgusting things I was forced to do for those boys at the orphanage. I had a creepy feeling that unnerved me for a while. Then sleep overcame me, sealing my eyes, deactivating my mind and putting my body to rest. I got up the next morning to see bright sunlight streaming through the window into our room. A bit nervous and unsure about what to do and what not to do, I came out of my room. I badly wanted to relieve myself. In the orphanage, we had to go to open fields for defecation. One hostel staff could sense my predicament and showed me the toilet with the required instructions regarding how to use it. That again was my first experience of using a toilet.

A SPARK IGNITED

The days that followed were certainly eventful in more than one way or another. During the first few days,

I explored everything, I had never seen or experienced before. Each day was a new day for me. I found everything fascinating; a new classroom, the dual desks and benches, rooms illuminated by electric bulbs. I moved around with that bright-eyed and bushy-tailed feeling that usually comes to one, undertaking a new adventure. My classmates were certainly more privileged than me. The classrooms bustled with the deep resonating voice of the teacher interacting with the students. With time, I gradually started forgetting the unfortunate inmates of the orphanage who were still languishing there with a vague hope for better days.

My performance at school during the first few days was disappointing. Not that my fellow batch mates were better than me. It was my shyness that put a brake on my efforts to prove my worth before a group of fiercely competitive students. I used to sit in one corner and listen to my teachers, watching them writing on the blackboard with their bodies slightly inclined and heads, all covered with chalk dust. Their dedication was amazing and so was their teaching skills. The school, the classroom, and the teachers helped me forget my suffering and the sense of deprivation, and they instilled within me the motivation to excel in life. I could never forget my mother's words, "Only you can put an end to our misery".

In the first terminal examination, I stood second in my class, surprising everyone. Some of my classmates even didn't know me. The boy whose position I usurped, pushing him back to third position was furious. However, I was happy that my classmates started treating me with some respect, even though they all knew something about my family background. Dhani Sir never missed an opportunity to visit me at least once every month. His presence worked as a kind of catalyst for me. Babu Bhai also came sometimes with some homemade snacks. Within a couple of years, he looked too old for his age. I had been to my home only thrice during the three years after my father's death. I had never noticed any visible improvement in our standard of living. My mother used to advise me not to worry about the affairs at home and focus hard on my studies.

In the final examination, I shocked everyone by securing the most coveted first position in my class. There was a small tremor in the school as this news spread rapidly among my classmates and teachers. Some viewed me as if, I had trespassed into a forbidden zone without any prior permission and the others treated me with the awe, that a malevolent deity gets in a village temple. I just basked in this newfound status of superiority.

For five long years, I was unbeatable, a star shining on the yonder sky. My teachers had high expectations from me and they kept growing after the completion of each year. I got a national scholarship in class seven and continued in the same school for four more years. The only change that took place in my career was being shifted to hostel no 1, meant for the senior boys. I stayed in a four-sitter room. My classmates and even the immediate seniors were seeking help from me in their studies.

Each year was a new year with a new goal, some new promises, and a year of hard work and perseverance. My destiny had set the momentum and I had to move forward, forgetting my bleak past. I took the class eleven board exams and passed with an impressive performance, securing 88 per cent and an all-Odisha eighth rank. My teachers were ecstatic. There was a small celebration at school. I was the lone student from the institution who had stormed into the prestigious top ten position in the board examination for the first time in the history of our school. But I was still very tense about my future. "What will happen when I land in the college of my choice? Will this scholarship money be enough to continue higher studies? Who will send me monthly pocket money? Who will be willing to engage a sixteen-year-old as a home tutor just because he has bagged a high rank in the state merit list? The only solution to my problem is getting my identity mortgaged. I need someone to hold my hand and lead me to my goal". I got mentally ready for the ultimate bargain. I knew I had a long way to go, holding a handful of uncertainties and fear in my hand……

PART-TWO

I, ME AND MYSELF

I am Rajiv, the narrator of a story of two individuals whose lives got intertwined at one point in time. Was it the design of providence or a mere coincidence? You need to know my perception and that's important before I tell you our story: the bond that was formed between me and Arun, the protagonist of this novel. I was brought up with so much love in my childhood that, one fine day, to my horror, I realised that love is a strange mental disorder that is often misconstrued as someone's unselfish affection for somebody. But my understanding of love is following the call of my own heart and doing things that my heart dictates me to do for someone. However, finding that someone can be as daunting as the fruition of an impossible dream. At times, I used to feel terribly intrigued in my attempts to understand why people are so obsessed with the idea of being in love as if, that's the only thing that makes life complete.

Living a compartmentalised life with one overpowering obsession was always difficult for me, as it is today. As a child, I always fancied living in a house, located in a place where the blue sky meets the blue sea, where I could fly like a bird, swim like a fish, and live in a burrow like a rabbit. Life was just an emancipating vision for me. I wanted to live life on my own terms and that primordial desire remained the only love of my life, if that is what love is.

Loving someone in a clichéd manner as an adolescent was a difficult accomplishment for me, more difficult than scuba diving with an untrained tourist: the excitement is marred by fear, anticipation, and inexperience.

One can, at best, get infatuated, have a crush on somebody or a wild fling. But that doesn't mean love. At times, love is used synonymously with care, duty, attachment, and attraction. But to me, it's a higher state, very rarely attainable. It's a deep gut feeling that comes from within. Love doesn't require any conscious effort. It just happens even before you realise you are in love. Love is a miracle in one's life, and miracles happen occasionally.

As a youngster, I spent two valuable years of my life smitten with my crush on one of my pretty batch mates who didn't even know me. She was a sweet girl with a pair of lovely dark blue eyes and a tender voice. She was not exactly that vivacious type, but she was elegant and graceful, a treat for the eyes of someone who barely had a chance in his secluded life to view the world before with all its bounties and glory. I was just a crazy teenager. Her lack of response, the remote prospect of ever connecting with her and the degree of unpredictability about the future of my dreams or desires hardly mattered to me. Like love, they were also emancipated from time and space. She vanished from my life one fine day, before I could comprehend what she meant to me. That night, I celebrated my failure with a few pegs of cheap whiskey and lots of alcohol induced tears. The next morning, I woke up with a heavy head. I thanked the girl for initiating me into the wonderfully intoxicating world of alcohol. The sense of nothingness was so sad yet fulfilling. But honestly, I couldn't feel the remotest feeling of being in love or being betrayed in love anywhere in my heart, save an all-consuming regret for wasting the precious time, that I should have utilised to study hard to make my father feel proud of his mediocre son, at least once in his life.

My feelings for her didn't vanish with time. It lingered within me as a precondition for living a complete life, I thought, I could never live without knowing what this entire experiment could mean to a man. It was not that, I didn't develop any crush on a woman later in my life. Women came and disappeared like faces on the silver screen, giving me my share of reveries and fantasies, sometimes a dopamine-driven physical manifestation that started from the brain and travelled downwards. I did not fall or rise in love because, with time, I realised that I had never been in love with anyone. Later on, I learnt to stay in my loveless mansion, where none, but people like me, could get entry. My friends and I kept ourselves completely preoccupied, exploring every experience prohibited, forbidden or considered a stigma by a group of people, who we unanimously disowned before they could disown us.

After being disappointed once, that too so badly at a tender age, when all calculations seemed to go wrong, I saw my friends, who knew my story, falling in love, sinking and suffering after being ditched in what they called love. But I always reserved my prudence and rarely poked my ugly nose into their love life. I wanted them to treat me as a case study and exercise some restraint when it came to falling or rising in love. They never did, nor did I go out of the way to hold them back and earn the tag of being ridiculed as a betrayed lover who turned into a misogynist just after one unsuccessful escapade. I decided to celebrate their success and mourn their failures with the same detached objectivity that one friend felt for another after he had a very narrow escape from a debacle called love.

Let me write my disclaimer: I always adore, respect and admire the woman for filling up the void in a man's life, for sacrificing her love and attachment for the people with whom she spends a sizable portion of her life before she takes the risk to gamble with her destiny, by tying a knot with someone, who she barely knows or in the best case scenario, knows too little to spend an entire life with him. But that is not love. In between love and friendship, I have always kept friendship above love. My friends always meant, and they still do, mean much more to me than mere loving persons who have given me company in this difficult journey of life and made it both worth living and worth dying. If I had ever fallen in love as a youngster with some people, then it was with my friends. It was a continuous affair of loving, unloving, fighting and then compromising, envying and admiring a bunch of youngsters within whom, someone like me with a lonely childhood had discovered the meaning of living a life that had always been tardy slow, dull and boring.

THE EVENING SKY AND THE CRESCENT MOON

I was also born in a small village. It was small in every respect. A small landmass, ringed by a river and a canal with less than thirty houses scattered in an uneven pattern and a thick cluster of foliage overhead through which sunlight often struggled to penetrate; that was my village. The denizens were simple, the demographic structure was uniform and the culture was ostensibly free from any complication or pretension. Most of the villagers were small-scale farmers and some were daily wage earners. My father was a teacher at a local government high school. We had a few acres of land, two bullocks and a domestic help to take care of the cultivation and help my parents by running some much-needed errands that they found difficult to handle.

The expression "far from the madding crowd and ignoble strife" sounded like an extended hyperbole, though my village was far away from the city. Although quarrels and strifes were not so uncommon, yet they were short-lived and easily forgettable. The purity and simplicity of the people, though defiled at times due to poverty and affliction, left an indelible impression on me as I grew up among them.

The houses were built of mud with thatched roofs overhead. Some of them were small enough to be called huts and some were large clay structures with elevated verandas and adjoining barns to preserve the annual harvests. There was a large rectangular plot of common area where small children were allowed to play during the afternoon. That was the only time when the entire village used to witness a pleasant commotion, created by the excited young kids. An eerie silence engulfed the entire village with the onset of the evening. All one could hear was the tinkling bells from the nearby temple and evening prayers sung by the children at home, followed by the hooting of owls, howling of dogs and moaning of jackals from the distant crematorium at regular intervals.

I was the fourth child of my parents. My mother had almost given up hope after giving birth to three girls. But both my parents treated them with love and care.

Normally in an orthodox rural household, a girl child was considered an unwanted addition to the family. When my mother conceived for the fourth time, she had to spend nine long months in uneasy anticipation and fear because my parents couldn't think of having a fourth daughter in the family and exhaust the remnants of their rapidly depleting resources.

I was born in our kitchen, which was the designated labour room during those days. A bamboo pole was fixed firmly in one corner, which the woman undergoing labour pain had to hold for support and relief from the excruciating pain. Normally an unskilled midwife was given the arduous task of childbirth. However, my father had hired the services of a staff nurse. He was vaguely hopeful that the fourth one would be a male child and destiny didn't disappoint him this time. My first cry brought more relief than happiness to the family on that quiet winter afternoon when the face of the setting sun turned purple with happiness and compassion for my poor mother. There was celebration all around. My cousin rushed to the nearby bazaar to buy sweets to be distributed among all our friends and relatives. My mother was lying in the dark labour room, dazed but happy. One kerosene lamp was burning on the top of the wooden lamp post, struggling to dispel the accumulated darkness with its feeble orange flicker surrounded by moths, who had sneaked in to see me before their routine self-immolation. A small child was crying in his mother's lap, eyeing the strange play of light and darkness with curiosity. But he was too young to notice the light on his mother's face, too young to think, understand and emote.

It was the beginning of the journey of an unknown human being from one opaque world to another.

My sisters took upon themselves the responsibility of bringing me up with unmixed love and care ever since the day I was born. As a hypochondriac since my childhood, I was treated with utmost care and caution. Overindulged and over-fondled by each one of them, I grew up to become an insensibly demanding spoilt brat, unwilling to compromise with my priorities at any point in time. Every woman is born with an innate maternal instinct that makes her an epitome of love and sacrifice, and my sisters were no exception. They became my mothers before they became my sisters. We didn't fight for parental love, for our rights. I meant the world to them and they were happy to forget all their dreams and ambitions so that their little brother could live without being neglected or deprived. None of them ever craved any reciprocation from their brother. I distinctly remember how my second sister used to carry me to school with her arms around me in a firm and tight embrace. She used to wait for me outside to take me back home after the final bell was rung. My mother was not keeping well most of the time. So, the responsibility of bringing me up rested completely on my sisters.

My father was a tall, good-looking man with a stern exterior and my mother was a complete contrast as far as appearance and temperament were concerned. She was short and demure, with an emaciated body and a sweet face. She was someone who could stir feelings of love even in an insensitive heart. But most of the time she was sick, her problems were more psychological than physical. As I grew up, I slowly started realising that she couldn't get the love and care from her in-laws, which she was getting in abundance from her parents, being their only child. It was difficult to live with a perennial sense of deprivation, an oppressive feeling of subjugation when one was treated like an alien in her in-laws' home, which was supposed to be her own home. Even after she became the mistress of the house, the shadows of her mental agony refused to leave her, taking her to the brink of depression. My sisters had seen the frozen sediments of sorrow in her eyes that she had never shared with anybody, not even with her daughters. My sisters had developed amazing adaptability and none of them wanted to put any pressure on her fragile mind. There were occasional eruptions of quarrel between my parents that sometimes threatened to disrupt the peace in our household. But my mother was always reclusive and each time she fought with my father, she had made it a habit to retreat to a self-created world of seclusion and remain stuck in her private world at least for a month or so. We were used to this syndrome. My father was a patient man. He allowed her this self-inflicted state of exile as long as she wished to stay in it and never bothered to interfere with her privacy with any pretentious protestation of remorse or repentance. He knew that any effort to alleviate her sorrows would further worsen the situation. Moreover, my mother's mind was like the subdued twilight, punctuated by intermittent play of darkness and light before night sets in to placate a restless world with a lullaby.

THE REAL AND THE ETHEREAL

As I grew up, I spent my childhood, hearing stories about ghosts and fairies from my mother and grandmother. They lived in my mind as my invisible neighbours. I sometimes conjured up visions of imaginary encounters with them. While going to school, I searched for them and tried to feel their elusive, ethereal existence. I sometimes narrated stories about spirits, demons and fairies, I had heard from my mother and grandmother to my friends, only to be scoffed at by their derisive laughter that sometimes shook the foundation of my belief in the existence of the supernatural. I started reading supernatural stories and fairytales at an early age without feeling scared. Sometimes at night, while staring at the thick foliage of the mango trees around our house, I was startled to see a few bright green eyes of some faceless entities whom, I was too willing to believe to be some supernatural beings residing on that tree. To my utter disappointment, one day, my mother told me that they were wild cats.

I had heard the creepy tale of a strange entity with a face that resembled a pig, who had turned the life of one poor young widow in my village into hell with his regular intrusion into her house in the dead of the night. Strangely, one day, the entire village got abuzz with the news of her pregnancy. Some stupid villagers believed that it could be the doing of the lecherous spirit: whereas all others believed it to be the sacrilegious outcome of a clandestine relationship. She had cooked up such a creepy story to keep people away from her home so that she could enjoy the company of her lover in the quietness of the night. Strangely the poor lady disappeared one morning and never came back. Her abrupt disappearance lent some credibility to the rumour about her extramarital affair. But there were a few who believed that she was abducted by the evil spirit who was regularly invading her home to take advantage of her helplessness and gratify his unfulfilled lust.

I had also heard about the spirit of the tamarind tree. The tree, enormous in size, stood majestically for decades on the sloppy ground the villagers regularly used to go down to the canal to take a bath in the morning. The old tamarind tree had cast a captivating spell on my young mind. I had heard hundreds of spooky stories from my grandmother, who was not so good at singing lullabies to a restless child, unwilling to stay put on his bed to enjoy an afternoon nap. In most of her stories, the spirit on the tamarind tree was a predominant entity, somewhat mysterious and scary for the unbridled imagination of a child. My grandmother was cunning, and she always succeeded in her clever manoeuvre to give me some fear-induced sleep, for a very short time though. The spirit of the tamarind tree squatted firmly on the self-inflicted closure of my impatient eyes that automatically fluttered open hearing the soft snores of my grandmother on a summer afternoon. Who was

I afraid of, the spirit or the repulsive perseverance of the nagging old lady to put me to sleep? I could never forget my helplessness while lying down passively beside her (pretending to be asleep) and visualising a personal encounter with the malevolent antagonist of my grandmother's incoherent, sleep-laden narrative.

The tamarind tree was a perpetual enigma for me. I was not as afraid of the invisible entity as I was of the scary hype that the ancestors of the gullible villagers had created long before I was born. How many of them had actually encountered him on one of those stilly nights on the dark and deserted road was not known. But we had accepted his ominous presence and his nocturnal exploits with an unquestionable conviction. The spirit of the tamarind tree evolved with time to become a cultural construct, with the roots challenging the vulnerability of the credulous villagers. Some concerned villagers had made a few abortive bids to send the spirit away with the help of some self-proclaimed *tantriks*, who were frequently coming to our village to perform exorcism whenever a young unmarried girl was found behaving in a rather weird manner. We were never allowed to watch any occult practice as spirits were deemed to be more contagious than a deadly virus. Sometimes, there were stories of stubborn apparitions surrendering to the magical power of the Tantrik, who imprisoned them in bottles and carried them home like a trophy.

Accepting paranormal stories as a part of reality that remains suspended in the twilight zone of truth, half-truth, and untruth had been a quintessential part of our childhood. They intruded freely into the realm of our fancy, our imagination, and our perception of a shapeless shape, inducing nightmares every now and then.

It was a hot summer day. I was returning from my school, which was barely two kilometres from my ancestral home. In those days, wearing slippers was also a luxury. Blisters were common manifestations on the tender feet of a child walking barefoot. I was feeling hungry and tired. I decided to take a shortcut to reach home early. The huge tamarind tree stood on the roadside: lush green, bushy, and laden with ripe tamarinds. I was virtually running to cross the forbidden zone, holding my breath for a while. The weight of the loaded canvas bag, and an old umbrella with a handle made of bamboo, made my homecoming a tedious exercise. While crossing the tamarind tree with my eyes partially closed out of fear, I heard someone calling me by my name. I stopped for a while and looked back.

Beneath the tree stood a man holding a sling in his hand. He was abnormally short and dark. But there was something in his voice that took all the fear away from my mind. He had a large protruding belly with a long white scar. He was wearing a homespun *gamchha.* He called me again and this time more tenderly. I dragged my reluctant steps to go near him. Perhaps he had cast a spell on me. " You are Dola's grandson? Ain't you?" He asked softly. I said, " Yes". He continued, "She is so fond of ripe tamarinds. She doesn't come here anymore. You tell her that Brahma Kaka has sent this for her. She will understand" I couldn't say anything. I grabbed the bag and started running. I could hear his last sentence, " Mitu, there is no spirit on this tree. Tell your grandmother that Brahma Kaka told you not to believe in these stupid stories."

I was running for my life, holding the pouch in my hand. His voice slowly became inaudible and dissolved with the ether. The sky, the air, the birds, and the muddy water of the canal might have heard the remnant of his words.

My grandmother heard the incident. Her face turned pale. She stood motionless on the door, holding the pouch in her trembling hands. I told her about the man I had met, his abnormally protruding belly and the long scar on his abdomen. That night, while sleeping beside her, I felt her arms entwined delicately around my slender frame. She had never held me like that before.

But I learnt one lesson, that I always keep in my mind: Spirits, if they exist, are not always malevolent entities with one mission on hand: to scare or harm innocent people. Spirits are not necessarily bereft of humanity. They are just the 'others' with their otherness, we never understand.

THE CAGED BIRD

Stories used to fascinate my young, immature mind. I started reading books at an early age. My father regularly borrowed books from his school's lending library. I finished reading the abridged versions of many world-famous classics by the time I was in class seven. But mere reading of books was not enough. I still remained a mediocre student, handicapped by my inability to do well in mathematics. I scored well in literature and social studies. But the surplus marks in these subjects couldn't get me a position in my class tests. The tag of mediocrity continued to haunt me till I was in class

XI. I was commuting on a bicycle to my school with my father with a stern and precise instruction to follow him. As a schoolboy, I found the freedom enjoyed by the children of my age group enviable. My movements and my freedom to do and not to do things were always restricted and regulated by my overprotective father.

I was allowed to play cricket only on Sunday afternoons and go out with my friends only for a couple of hours on holidays, only after furnishing authentic information about our destination, the purpose of our visit and the number of hours we were planning to spend there. Even the safety and security issues were given priority before granting me permission. My father didn't know that I was gradually turning into a rebel with suppressed anger and frustration. I was a victim of oppressive magnanimity that curtailed my freedom, dampened my spirit and overpowered my desires. I was like a caged bird, who could see the sky through the bars of his cage but never fly since its wings were trimmed.

I was just waiting for an opportunity to fly away to the blue sky, feel the sun, the rain, the darkness and the light, the moon and the stars. I was yearning for freedom, unbridled freedom and I was getting ready to have it at any cost.

It's not as unnatural for an adolescent to yearn for freedom as it is for the parents to be discerning while allowing youngsters the license to do things, they love to do because no one knows their child better than the parents. So, the trust deficit, when it comes to granting freedom to the children, is not so uncommon and similarly, a corresponding reaction from a child who feels deprived of the pleasures or funs that some of his friends are having, becomes imminent. Nobody is more concerned for your child than you. That's why you decide what's best for your child. You thrust your prescriptive 'do's and don'ts' on their head as a protective guardian, while your children consider it an act of invasion of their privacy, which they strongly feel they are entitled to have, as they become teenagers.

That was exactly the case with my father. He had grappled with my health issues right from the day I was born, and as I kept growing up, my health complications kept rising like the mercury in a barometer on a hot summer day. My father always had doubts about the chances of me recovering completely and becoming a normal, healthy boy like the rest of my friends. The memories of all those sleepless nights he had spent beside my bed kept haunting him even after I started showing promising signs of being normal. He was always cautious while dealing with issues that could possibly make me ill once again, issues like granting permission to watch theatres or operas in open areas, playing outdoor games that require a lot of stamina, travelling alone to a distant place, etc. His unwillingness to allow me to lead a normal life, which most of my friends were leading, made me turn hostile towards my father. I had never tried to find out why he was so reluctant to let me lead a life that would put on him neither any physical exhaustion nor financial pressure.

I simply wanted to break free and escape into a world, where there wouldn't be a master to regulate my life with his diktats. It didn't matter, how useful they were to me. I wanted to be on my own, chase my dreams, roam freely in my world, and not pay any heed to stigmas, taboos, inhibitions or prohibitions. I knew I was not a brilliant student. I was happy with my mediocrity. I had set my priorities long before my father could have an inkling of what was going on in my mind.

THE LURE OF THE BLUE SKY

I passed my class eleven board examination, scoring a bare minimum of 60% of marks. Though I was not ecstatic, I was not very unhappy. My father was certainly disappointed, but my mother was happy. She didn't want to let me go anywhere for higher studies. Her unwillingness to stay away from me at times was so apparent because she was so bad at hiding things, almost incapable of faking an emotion or talking diplomatically to someone to avoid any dispute. She was timid but frank and outspoken. She was what she was, and all she had wanted from her life was not to part with me as long as she would remain alive. My father was also not too enthusiastic to let me stay in a far-off city just to pursue my studies. It was not that he was not serious about the career of his mediocre son, but my health problems always posed a threat to any ambitious decision he could have taken to plan my career as he might have wished it to be. Moreover, my result became a huge dampener, and he agreed with my mother to get me admitted to a nearby college where I could commute daily from home. That was the final assault on my dreams, my destiny and my destination by my overprotective parents. I finally decided to retaliate for the first time in my life.

I was desperate to leave home and stay in a hostel. I had applied accordingly for my admission into intermediate classes at an illustrious institution like

Ravenshaw College, though I was not very optimistic about getting a seat there. My father had made up his mind to put me in a local college. The idea of studying there was as repugnant to me as sitting idle at home, bearing the tag of being a useless teenager. I decided to stand solidly on my ground and defend my decision to study at a good college, where I could at least try to salvage the battered ego of my father. He had always been stubborn, and this time, I was obstinate. For a week or so, my sisters witnessed a high-voltage family drama, dealing with a clash between a father and a son, who had never spoken a word in disagreement to his loving yet dominating father. My mother's last trick to blackmail me made my grounds slippery. But I was not ready to give up so soon. It was a do-or-die situation for me, and I was determined not to budge an inch, no matter what tools my parents had in their toolbox to nail my dreams.

Finally, my sisters came to my rescue. They had seen me suffering like a rabbit, entrapped in a snare. None of them could approve of the idea of me rotting in a place that held no hope. They had passed out from the same college where my father wanted to put me and were mentally getting ready to spend the rest of their lives as non-descript housewives, marrying someone our father would choose for them, a choice based on our father's ability, social status and convenience. There was nothing they could do, save accepting the decision of the great patriarch, the greatest well-wisher-cum-saviour of our family. But they could not bear to see their only brother sailing in the same boat. They fought for me the most decisive battle of their lives to impart momentum to my ongoing agitation to let me make my own decision.

My parents were certainly not ready for such united resistance. They had never seen my sisters mumbling out even one word in disagreement. This open rebellion forced them to rethink and reconsider their decision. My mother was more insistent than my father. She had never been so vocal, supporting any decision that my father took. But she was certainly not ready to part with me, and when my father was helplessly tossing about in between the two horns of a dilemma, my mother was busy inventing a series of excuses to prevent what, according to her, was the beginning of a disaster. Finally, my father declared a temporary ceasefire with a consoling announcement that the final decision would be taken only after my selection for admission. He said a bit sarcastically, "One can think of a name for his son only after having a wife". I felt hurt, but kept mum. However, after a few days, I received a letter of confirmation from Ravenshaw College regarding my admission into intermediate classes in the Arts stream. I was ecstatic and my parents were disappointed. For the first time in my life, I started believing in the cliched proverb, "Hope is the dream of a waking man".

The next few days were spent on having elaborate discussions about the pros and cons of staying away from home with a group of youngsters who could be of my age. The chance of a gullible country lad like me falling into bad company and going astray was one deterrent that kept my father on the back foot. Moreover, my health issues, sleeping alone in the hostel, and not getting proper care or medical attention were a few more grey areas to be explored by my over-concerned parents. The views of my relatives were also sought, which were mostly negative, owing to their jealousy or concern for me. Negative remarks, discouraging statements, and sly mockery of my ambition swelled around me like a river in flood. Yet I was determined to swim across this river of negativity to land on the bank and trudge along to the world of my dreams. Their resistance made me more resilient; their protest made me more belligerent. During all those days, I had alienated myself from my surroundings and built a world for myself in another world beyond the reach of my parents.

That was the moment in my life, the moment of crisis that made me what I became later in my life. That was the beginning of my journey into a dark nothingness that looked like a mirage in the desert to a hallucinating youngster. But frankly speaking, at that stage, I had no other choice available to me. Years of repression had hardened my heart. It was not my ambition, my aspiration, or my vision to explore a viable career option that propelled me to quit my home. I badly needed an escape route and I found one. At last, my father agreed to get me admitted to Ravenshaw. Keeping aside all those ifs and buts, optimism and doubts. I got ready to take a plunge into a future that awaited me.

PART-THREE

HE AND ME: ONE SKY, TWO EARTHS

The day we met, a bond was formed. I swear, it's not going to be a story celebrating friendship, love, and sacrifice, nor is it about disappointment, rivalry and mistrust. It's much more complex and intricate than any story written about friendship. It's the story of two youngsters, meeting in a novel setting, staying together under one common roof, getting to know each other slowly but steadily with time and liking and disliking each other intermittently. Two different entities with two completely different backgrounds, outlooks and ideologies, bound together in an inextricable affiliation, wrought by a capricious destiny, landed that day in their land of youth and dreams.

Arun was a bright young boy and I was just an average student. He was ambitious and I was too callous to nurse any ambition with some seriousness. He had a dream to fulfil and I had none. He had a dark past buried within his heart and I had nothing to hide. I was absolutely candid when it came to sharing my childhood afflictions and denial of freedom at home with anyone whom I could find a bit affable or friendly. He was fighting with the demon within himself, and I was just happy to enjoy the newfound freedom without any remorse or guilt or any kind of accountability. He was not like me and I was not like him. Yet we liked each other without any precondition or expectation.

We were put up in a huge dormitory, which could accommodate thirty-six inmates, all newcomers from the same batch. There were four ceiling fans, hanging from the ceiling, whirring incessantly day in and day out without showing any sign of fatigue. In a huge room measuring 40 ft x 40 ft, they barely succeeded in diffusing the heat and humidity during summertime. The room was fitted with eight hundred-watt electric bulbs at all strategic dark corners, emitting reddish harsh light day and night. Switching off the light during the day was not possible because of the pervasive presence of thick darkness even during the day. At night, we had to keep at least two bulbs on to find a passage to the bathrooms, which were located 100 meters from our dormitory. Huge, claustrophobic, and awe-inspiring, the dormitory had everything that youngsters could detest most. Having some privacy was a foregone conclusion. Some meritorious students built small cells using their bedsheets tied to the wooden T's fixed permanently to every bed to hang the mosquito nets. There was no dearth of mosquitoes in our dorm. An army of tiny mosquitoes used to swarm around us with aggressive intent every evening to fill their filthy tummy with our blood. Ironically, I used one of them later to fulfil one of my ludicrous missions.

There was a long corridor leading to the quarters of the warden and hostel superintendent, fitted with black iron railings to prohibit our entry into the huge quadrangle surrounded by four majestic rows of buildings in a rectangular pattern. Two of these were used as Arts block and Science block and the other two were used as boys' hostels facing east and west and therefore named East Hostel and West Hostel. If you visit Ravenshaw College now, you won't see any major structural change, though the campus has been renovated after the college was upgraded to a university. During morning hours, we used to roam on that secluded corridor, looking at pretty girls treading upon those red-bricked roads that intersected each other at the centre, where the famous sundial clock was strategically placed by the precocious architect who designed the building.

Occasionally, some of our adventurous friends used to pass one or two lewd remarks, which were reciprocated by the victim with matching aggression and disdain. That was fun for us. At night, we used to fantasise about our sensual proximity to them in our self-created private dreams.

Arun was so much unlike us. When we were wasting our time on meaningless gossip, he was invariably on his chair, reading a book or writing something with an enviable concentration or lost in deep contemplation. On some evenings, he was found sitting in the study centre, when we were slipping out of the hostel campus to watch movies. He had never skipped a lecture or an assignment and never neglected his homework. He had come with a mission, and everything that a young lad of his age would like to do assumed little significance in his life. I had never seen someone so sharp, yet so detached, so objective yet so unassuming and someone who was one amongst us, yet so much above us.

Why Arun started liking me remained a perpetual enigma to me. He had never endorsed my way of looking at things, nor did he try to emulate any of my qualities, which sometimes a few of my classmates found fascinating. Perhaps he liked my eloquence, my frankness and my ability to reach out to people or break the ice between two youngsters clashing with each other to justify their inflated egos. I was simply a good troubleshooter, amiable and convincingly logical. Oratory had always been my strength, and he, being inordinately reticent, gradually started adoring my articulation skills, my ability to make friends, and the deftness with which I was settling disputes. I had helped him once when one of our friends with a robust frame and formidable appearance threatened to smash his skull when Arun called him an arrogant knave. I intervened to negotiate a compromise between both of them without being biased towards anyone. It was a good job, cleanly done. He remained grateful to me for doing it so well.

I always disliked his idiosyncrasies, the conviction that he could never be wrong. He was shy but not afraid to give his views on any contentious matter and stuck to them with an irritating rigidity that made him a bit unpopular among a bunch of talented students. They often found it difficult to accept his intellectual superiority and the bold assertion of his views, which were sometimes fiercely emphatic and ingeniously innovative. But there was something about his personality, that I always found so adorable. I was always with him to defend him, protect him and make others acknowledge his precocity, grudgingly though. Every genius is invariably eccentric.

ROMANCING A NEW WORLD

Life at Ravenshaw was incredibly exciting. The professors were no ordinary mortals. We had the highest respect for many of them. Their electrifying presence in the classroom, the maverick delivery of lectures, the sophistication of their attire, and even the cars they used: I found everything about them fascinating. In the vast sprawling campus with a tennis court and four huge hostels, three of which were boys' hostels and the one was the romantic abode of our sweet, elegant lady loves who didn't have even a shred of premonition about our secret crush on them, life became an endless adventure, an experiment with the probabilities of attainments and failures. We roamed around the campus from morning to evening, exploring its exquisite splendour. Our evening get-togethers were the most exciting parts of our lives when we used to sit on the small cement bench in front of the psychology department and gulp down cups of tea amidst endless animated conversations about the pretty girls and their secret anatomies. There were discussions about the all-important yet unproductive college politics. Every morning at 9 a.m., most of us gathered in front of the psychology department (which boasted of the treasure of having the highest number of pretty girls) to have a glimpse of those nymphs going in and coming out of the department. But all our adventures were mostly confined to stealing glances and passing naughty but innocuous remarks under our breaths. We were the proud boarders of the illustrious hostels housed within that esteemed temple of learning.

The word 'we' referred to a group of some twenty-odd students from one age group but with glaring dissimilarities. Some of our friends were rich, some came from middle and lower-middle-class families, and some were poor. But all of us had one common agenda: to explore all the pleasures of life without seeking validation from those, who didn't belong to our league. We were all unacknowledged exponents of permissive education, an inclusive culture that was not opposed to a reasonable degree of anarchy. But Arun was not like us. He preferred to spend his time reading and rereading books, attending lectures and mixing pleasure and perseverance judiciously. He was with us, yet so far away from us. He had never sought validation from any one of us, because he knew he was on the right track and a slight deviation could be detrimental to the greater cause that brought him to this place.

The first two years passed like a dream. Being teenagers, we couldn't completely neglect our studies because the fear of not doing adequately well in the final examination to ensure a permanent berth in a degree course with the honours of our choice always loomed large. Facing my father with a poor performance report and enduring his petulance with my head hung and eyes lowered became a recurring nightmare. I could not afford an unceremonious expulsion from the lofty institution and subject my poor self to a series of indignities in the form of taunting remarks from my father, who was never keen to put me in the hostel. I became a little bit more serious towards the fag end of the second academic session. I focused on my preparations, which were almost in shambles due to a year-long thoughtless negligence of studies and crazy pursuit of whims, that always acted as deterrents to one's preparation.

Once, I had a misadventure when I tried to remove the railing of one of the windows of my room so that I could sneak into my hostel with my friends after watching a midnight show in a theatre. And the inevitable happened. The hostel clerk caught me red-handed while I was halfway through the narrow gap between the two iron railings, and the very next day, the furious warden was about to expel me from the hostel, a disaster I could avert with tearful protestation and a vow not to repeat any such misadventure in future. The warden was moved for a while, being deceived by my innocent look and, to my great relief, forgave me and my friends. We became extremely careful in the days to follow, being contented and contained with a few covert operations to execute our mischievous plans to defy the stringent rules of the hostel without being noticed. A few months before the final examination, to my horror, I realised how precariously I was placed and how much effort I had to put in to make amends. I stopped visiting movies, spending time with my friends, illicitly purchasing marijuana for consumption at night and concentrated hard on my studies. However, I couldn't give up smoking cigarettes and the nocturnal mission of slipping away from my hostel at night to sip tea at the railway station.

But Arun was rock solid, focused like a hermit. He knew he had a job in hand, and he had to get it done to escape from the labyrinthine complications of life. Most of the time, he was found glued to the wooden chair, reading reference books, nodding his head in a queer gesture and smiling slyly. He was fond of a particular girl but was always shy to let her know his tender feelings towards her. We had played a few pranks by writing letters and posing as the girl he was in love with. But he was intelligent enough to understand our design and shrewd enough to foil our bids to have some fun at his cost.

I, on the other hand, had my regular flings. I was too shy to flirt with a girl. But there was absolutely no problem in finding somebody attractive, liking her without any hope of being reciprocated, having sweet thoughts or feelings about her, and gradually forgetting her after finding someone more attractive or someone attainable and getting lost in the process of repeating the same cycle with the same results. My fantasies were private, uninhibited, wild, uncensored. I never shared my feelings with anyone. All my love stories had one common end; being a silent or an unknown admirer. I was happy because I never believed in fixities and finalities. Inside the campus, the ambience was always ripe for an unexpected tryst with someone known or unknown. We all knew anyone could fall in love with someone any day and write their own love or lust story.

THE CRUELLEST MONTH

We took the final examination in April. Later in my life, I understood why Eliot had called April the cruellest month. For more than a month, I was on a painful sabbatical from my semi-bohemian life. My friends were also amused to see me at my desk with so much seriousness. But no one knew, it was a premeditated effort, a small sacrifice just to renew my license to freedom. During the summer vacation, we went home, overburdened by our insecurities. Arun knew he would make it. But he was not very excited about going home. Despite being his best friend, I knew very little about his family life. Even the fact that he had spent a few years in an orphanage was not known to me until he decided to confide in me when he was infatuated with a girl whose lukewarm reciprocation had left him shaken. He told me the story of his past one night when he was getting mentally ready to close the chapter of his unrequited love story.

I had to stay at home for nearly two months, waiting desperately for my result to come. Of course, my father was more than understanding. And my mother was obsessed with making those two months the most memorable days of my life, bestowing all her love and care and trying to impress me with her culinary expertise, which was eclipsed so far by my elder sister, who was in charge of cooking till her marriage. For my mother, this was just the right opportunity to impress her only son, and from morning till night, she was busy cooking one thing or the other; all of them were exceptionally mouthwatering. I put on a few kilos of weight. But good food was no compensation for the freedom I had got accustomed to during those two eventful years of my life.

In July, the university published our results. Arun got the second intra-university rank, and to my surprise, I scored seventy percent in my examination. I had never expected to do so well. Perhaps the examiners who had evaluated my answers were either mad or careless. A seat in Ravenshaw in a degree course became a certainty for me. My result made my father proud and my mother and sisters happy. For me, it was a renewal of the pass through the gateway of heaven.

I got a letter from him after the publication of our results. He was disappointed with his performance. He had hoped to top the list, but that didn't happen. We didn't know then about the vicious lobby that operated in the university administration. The list of meritorious students was tampered with every year to accommodate the undeserving son or daughter of a university professor in the top slot. So, the slide down was inevitable. He was happy for me because I had done reasonably well with minimal effort. That was how he had summed up, "I know so little about you, and I feel so sorry for so grossly underestimating you". In fact, the reverse was true. But those two lines worked as a kind of stimulant for me. I was determined to do better in my final degree examination, a resolution that could never bear the seal of destiny.

AN EXPERIMENT, GONE ASTRAY

"Love has always been an enigma to all teenagers. Why specify teenagers? One may say with conviction that we still have reasonable doubts in our minds about understanding love, interpreting it, and explaining to others what exactly love is and how it is different from infatuation, crush, and fling. To put it in short, love is a serious affair, and all others are casual manifestations that go into oblivion with time. As a student of literature, I was familiar with Rumi, Gibran, Lawrence and many notable authors and their views on love, but I was still confused when it came to understanding love. Ironically, even without understanding love,

I had written at least a hundred love letters to a girl on behalf of my friend Vikash, when he hopelessly fell in love with a schoolgirl. The eloquent pronouncement of love in the letters I wrote helped him win the love of the girl, which at one stage seemed to be an impossible proposition".

When most of my friends were having their noble or ignoble romantic escapades, I was in a state of dilemma, asking myself the question, "Is what they are doing, worthwhile?" It was not that I had never felt tempted to venture into that risky terrain to try my luck, which had always been erratic in awarding me punishment or reward in all my endeavours. For example, when I was a second-year student, I noticed a pretty girl standing modestly on the threshold of the classroom and humbly seeking the permission of my teacher to allow her to attend his lecture 15 minutes after its scheduled commencement. The grumpy teacher allowed her to enter the class with a mild warning bordering on the zone of a sly reprimand. Her humility impressed me. I started following her discreetly for two long years without giving her a chance to have the remotest doubt about my intention. I didn't have any remorse that, she knew nothing about me except that, I was one of her classmates, ordinary and inconspicuous from all angles.

I was simply content to loiter a few yards away from her with my shadowy presence. She was somebody who I fondly remembered for a long time as my first romantic interest. I may sound ridiculous, but when some of my friends were smitten with the love of one girl or another and writing passionate letters to them dipped in their blood, I devised an ingenious technique to replicate their feat without hurting my poor limbs. I allowed a mosquito to suck my blood, and when its little tummy got full of my blood, I slapped it hard with my palm, which was in readiness ever since the mosquito sat on my other hand. It was a bloody insect sacrifice, and I wrote her name on one of my books with the blood I had ingeniously retrieved from the unsuspecting slain mosquito. However, I didn't flaunt it before my friends with the fear of being ridiculed for my cowardice. But I was never ashamed of it. At no point in time, could the sweet, innocent girl ever rule over my mind as an all-consuming passion or obsession. My long list of priorities rationally precluded any obsession, that would interfere with my freedom. But the day I got the news of her marriage, I felt a strange sadness within me. It was not the shame of rejection; because rejection always comes only after acceptance. Nevertheless, there was a void in my heart that day, a disturbing one, the void that unsettled me for a few days. For the first time in my life, I gulped down two pegs of whisky and came back to my hostel room, tottering all the way and using swear words with despicable eloquence. That was my experiment with love, which ended much before it had begun.

A NEW ADDRESS

Those were the two most decisive years of my life, the years that could make or break me as an individual by turning me into somebody or nobody. No one knew my truant destiny better than me. But the tragic indoctrination, that transformed me into a bohemian with an unshakable belief in the theme of Carpe Diem, was the beginning of my downfall. I was given accommodation in another hostel, located in one extreme corner of the campus, just behind the college playground. I was devastated because the selector considered my antecedents while allotting a hostel seat, not the marks I had scored in my final pre-university examination. My only consolation was that Arun was also put in the same hostel despite securing a rank in the same examination. The crime for this expulsion from one of the prestigious hostels of the campus was his occasional appearance on the corridor during power cuts at night and calling the superintendent with offensive adjectives, which was reported to his highness by some of his spies amongst us, who were too keen to remain in his good book.

Both of us shifted to our new destination, nursing the grudge of being 'more sinned against than sinning'. We were destined to be there. I was disunited from Vikash, Rasik and Raju, who were equal accomplices in most of my joint 'exploits' because that was what, I had done all through my college days. I was raving and ranting, expressing my angst against those who lived life with passion, but without conviction, but still got away with the providential leniency. Arun was cool. He would console me very often, quoting lines from Milton's Paradise Lost: "Mind is its own place, and in itself can make a heaven of hell, a hell of heaven". When he was getting ready to make his own heaven, I, the obnoxious hell boy, was ready to negotiate with the devil to get access to the forbidden pleasures of my choice.

I built my own rendezvous and invited only those who shared the same mental wavelength with me. We boozed, smoked, read pornographic literature, and looked for all possible avenues to do what our orthodox society considered taboos in the 1980s.

Arun was more focused on his goal. He wanted to excel, to scale the height of the sky and find a place for himself high up, somewhere in the bright blue sky. He was unhappy with me and wanted to mend my lifestyle and be my saviour. I was too adamant to allow him to interfere in my life, however benign his intention might have been. I took my own road, the road leading to the darkness, which I had thought was light for me. But we didn't part ways. We still shared a cosy emotional affinity. In my time of crisis, he was with me, and during his time of crisis, I was with him.

THE UNHOLY TRINITY

In the new hostel, which was aptly named The New Hostel as it was built almost forty years after the two old hostels, three strange persons barged into my life like a sudden advent of rain on fierce summer days, filling my heart with joy, a stray dog feels when it finds a few others, equally deprived, loathed and ill-treated like him. They were senior to me by at least two years. But this so-called seniority never intervened with the depth of our relationship. They had an ungrudging admiration for me, though I didn't know where they got it from, and I became their master while playing the role of a loyal protégée. Three of them were from remote villages, having very little pretensions and absolutely no illusions about their class and position. From morning till evening, I had only one fascinating preoccupation: moving around the campus with them and exploring every inch of it with no worries, no ambitions and no ennui. I was their friend, mentor and much indulged spoilt younger brother.

We were bound to one another by one common thread: economically weak, which brought us under one umbrella and liberated us from all moral and social inhibitions. We sometimes struggled to buy a cup of tea for ourselves, though all four of us were avid tea addicts. I was a bit privileged because I used to have my lunch and dinner at the hostel mess; whereas they were hostel outcasts after their post-graduation. Sometimes, I had to become a proud money lender just to arrange a delayed lunch or an almost substandard dinner for their starving bellies. Their misfortune sometimes made me think about my fortune, which had always existed in the form of an invisible deity in the darkest sanctorum of a mysterious village temple.

One day, it was pouring down heavily, and most of the boarders were in their respective rooms, enjoying the dampness with a hot cup of tea or a plate of *pokodas* lifted fresh from a hot cauldron. But I was standing in a narrow corridor of the botany department with my three loving friends, trying to devise an easy way to arrange the cheapest dinner for them. Finally, we agreed to cook our dinner in the dilapidated structure of a half-deserted hostel meant exclusively for a section of underprivileged students. We purchased some rice, dal, edible oil, onion, red chillies, and spices. When it came to buying vegetables, all of us found our pockets empty. But that could never chill down our tempo. Instantly, the eldest of the three climbed on a low wall and started plucking papayas from the plantation of the Botany Department. When the mission was about to be accomplished, the watchman came and raised an alarm. This intrusion infuriated my friend, who suddenly lost his cool and started throwing all the papayas at the petrified guard. The guard carried the windfall gains to home happily. That day, they had to sleep without food, and so did I because of my commitment to provide them with their dinner and my failure to do so.

We had nothing in our life to boast of except a deep sense of contentment, and the paucity of material prosperity or success could never dampen our spirit, because, those things never existed in our scheme of things. From morning till evening, life to us was a fluttering butterfly, and we never got tired of chasing it, though we never came close to it in any possible way. Frustration, sadness, and jealousy were to us all concepts or unpractised theories that existed in another terrestrial, and we were miles away from them. Small happiness, never measured, though, kept us preoccupied in our poor little world. Not that we never had any heartbreak or a pang, but they were not shattering enough to destabilise us, shake our precious equilibrium or throw us out of the orbit of a wonderful make-believe world.

When one of my senior pros was ditched in love, he cried like a child throughout the night. But the very next day, he sold the ring his girlfriend had given him on one rare occasion and threw a party in a nearby Dhaba to make a pompous celebration of his break off. I had never seen him taking her name from the next day. I was always critical of teenage lovers and could never fancy the idea of trying my luck in that forbidden zone. We need one relationship in life, and that relationship should be all-encompassing, endearing and strong, based on understanding and care. We were lucky enough to have that.

"Life is a maze, a mysterious quagmire with all plenitude and poverty. But we have to make it an easy exercise, read it as a simple, lucid poem and play it as an absorbing game, full of excitement but no jealousy or rivalry." My unholy trinity taught me this precious life lesson.

ON BEING A SILENT SPECTATOR

I remember Shankar, the man who sold vegetable and mutton chops at the college and hostels. Never in my life have I come across such yummy vegetable chops or mutton chops. Shankar had a workshop at Professor Para, and it was his family business. The much-awaited footsteps of Shankar were heard along the hostel corridor in the afternoon when the tired inmates were enjoying an afternoon nap. We could afford to buy his chops once in a blue moon. Our wealthier counterparts in the hostel were his regular customers. With a meagre pocket money granted to us by our parents, we were mostly dependent upon the generosity of the two biscuit sellers, Rama and Padia. Both of them used to come to our hostel in two separate time slots to sell cookies (then known as biscuits) to the boarders. Most of us were from lower middle-class families. But I had never seen Rama and Padia having any hesitation while giving us biscuits on credit, even though they had no valid reason to trust us as reliable customers when it came to repaying the cumulative credit. Both of them were living in a slum adjacent to the campus. One morning, the wristwatch of a boarder mysteriously disappeared from his cupboard, and one of his friends alleged that he had seen Padia sneaking into the victim's room just the afternoon before this incident. Most of the boarders got agitated and started beating the unsuspecting poor man. Some of them tied Padia to a wooden chair. Nobody was ready to listen to his side of the story, his helpless, tearful protestation. Padia was beaten mercilessly. How could someone be treated so savagely? Some boarders pounced upon the tin box containing the cookies and took as many as they could. I was standing there silently and cursing myself for not being able to help Padia. For a while, I felt ashamed to be a boarder of a hostel that had been providing accommodation to the cream of the students of this state.

What happened to Padia was unfortunate. I could never buy the story that a man like him could steal a wristwatch. Even if he was guilty, that was certainly not the way to treat him. Did someone deserve to be treated with so much brutality? What about those boys who took advantage of the situation and robbed a poor vendor? The tears in his eyes kept haunting me for days.

Padia stopped coming to our hostel after that incident. But I could not stop hating myself for being a silent spectator when a poor guy was so badly mauled just on the basis of someone's testimony.

THE DARK BUTTERFLY

Arun was quite popular in his honours group. Every year, many bright students used to opt for political science as their honours. Some of them had cracked the prestigious civil service examination, and some had joined colleges affiliated to Delhi University later in their lives. His honours mates knew his potential to crack the civil service. There was another tall, lanky boy who was also a civil service aspirant. He was amazingly well-read, an eloquent debater and a creative writer. The academic ambience in the department was good. You get a chance to grow, when there is healthy competition among students. Very often, boys and girls sat in small groups to discuss Karl Marx, Hobbes, or Locke. Arun was shy but incisive and logical. His views were restrained but never shallow. He was often flanked by girls who were eager to take his input. There was a girl called Ruby who had developed a certain degree of proximity with Arun.

Ruby was our batchmate. We studied in one college for four long years. During the first two years, Ruby was never our friend, she was just someone we knew by her appearance. Ruby stormed into his life when we were final-year students. She wasn't exactly beautiful in a conventional way, but attractive for reasons best known to a boy of her age. Ruby didn't have a steady boyfriend, but she had enough friends from both sexes with whom she could hang around in the snack bars, video parlours and sometimes in parks. We often discussed Ruby when we were with our close buddies in the privacy of our congested hostel rooms.

Ruby's father was a tailor. Ruby used to introduce herself as the daughter of a fashion designer. He had a swanky shop in the heart of the city and an indisputable reputation for designing the best suits and trousers for men. During those days, the word fashion designer had an aura, that could elicit a quaint mixture of admiration and awe from a group of country-bred lads, who had never seen anyone beyond a bespectacled old tailor sitting alone on a wooden cabin with an Usha sewing machine, his hands and legs frantically busy with a piece of cloth, enduring silently the bites of the cruel needle, attached to the clinking and clanking old machine. But Ruby's father was a fashion designer, and fashion designing to us was all about introducing new trends in a city that was still held in captivity of our precious age-old tradition and custom. Ruby's father was the pioneer, who emancipated the city from the clutch of orthodox outlook with his innovative dress design that included funky shirts and jeans. Anything fashionable had to be worn and exhibited with pride and splendour. Ruby's father liberated a generation from the constraints of being dressed in formal wear, that didn't disturb the aesthetic sense of the prudish parents.

Unlike many of us, Ruby was the privileged product of a reputed public school in the city. She had that uncanny exuberance only a few youngsters from her class had. Ruby had everything a young girl of her age could dream of. But Ruby was an enigma to all of us because eighteen-year-old Ruby was never seen with a boy who we could call her lover. We often stretched our imagination, unleashed our fancy and applied the theory of probability to discover Ruby's secret lover, if she had one.

I was not very happy with Arun's newfound interest in Ruby. One could call it my jealousy or my possessiveness. I was not sure about the conflicting emotions I had whenever I found them together. They were not behaving like lovers. But I was still very apprehensive, to be honest, a bit scared, because she certainly didn't belong to our league. She was a girl from another world, smart, flamboyant, intelligent, polished and confident. They were poles apart. I had never seen her trying to flirt with him or with any other young man I knew. But I knew my friend. I knew how vulnerable he was. Ruby was the first girl trying to get closer to him, and that thought was unsettling for me.

I had sometimes seen them sitting together in a deserted classroom, discussing some topics seriously. The glint of seriousness in Ruby's eyes was a bit disturbing because she was sitting there with the seriousness of a learner, not like an enticed beloved. Her devotion was directed more towards the content of the speaker than his persona. Was she manipulating the susceptibility of my friend by feigning her admiration for him, or was she genuinely impressed by his intellect? I didn't have the slightest clue. I was desperately looking for an opportunity to express my reservations about his questionable affiliation with Ruby, but I couldn't get any chance. I was gathering all my courage to exercise my pre-emptive right to save my friend from any unforeseen emotional turbulence. I was ready to be the proverbial bad man to prevent a highly risky romantic debacle, even at the cost of our friendship. I was ready to tell him that Ruby was not the right girl, even in the best-case scenario, to be his friend. She was like a dark butterfly, beautiful but sinister. I wanted to show him the mirror, knowing pretty well it might have a damaging consequence as far as my relationship with him was concerned.

THE FAILED ATTEMPT

One Sunday evening, when I had nothing much to do, I decided to talk to Arun. But I still didn't have the courage to hurt him. That day, I had to spend the last twenty bucks in my pocket to buy a quarter of cheap whisky. That was the last quarter of the month, with four more days to go. Spending the remnants of my pocket money on buying stuff like alcohol was a sin, but I didn't have any regret. I emptied the bottle, standing under a tree in a relatively darker place and practically staggered to my hostel with a job in hand.

Luckily, he was sitting on the parapet close to his room and inhaling the freshness of the evening air. When I saw him sitting alone, I was delighted. I shouted at him from a distance. That was how we used to show our fondness towards our friends with excessive and unreasonable use of swear words, a usual practice found in every hostel. They were not metaphorically abusive but rather a bold and indiscriminate manifestation of affection towards a friend. We were all used to the trend, and no one took any offence in being addressed with such abominable slang. Sometimes, such unrestrained public use of slang put some of our friends in embarrassing situations, especially when their visiting parents were around. But that was how hostel life was, punctuated by obnoxious habits and practices, and nobody seemed to mind that.

I staggered all the way, shouting fondly at him. He was a bit shocked to find me in an inebriated state in the evening, which, according to many, was not the right time to drink. I sat near him clumsily and held his left hand. Then I started tottering, "Look, Arun, you are not just a friend to me. You are my brother, my mentor, my saviour. I am staying in this hostel only because of you". He shook his hand gently and asked me with concern in his eyes, "Please cut it short; I know what I mean to you and you to me. Why this confession in such a state at this hour? Go to your room and get some rest. We will talk after dinner". I didn't have any patience to listen to him. I blurted out emphatically this time,

"Arun, don't interrupt me today. If I do not speak, my heart will burst like a balloon. Let me speak. Just listen to me patiently". I was trying to make my utterance coherent, though the effect of alcohol was gradually snapping apart the intended thread of conversation, obliterating fragments of my memory and making it difficult for me to recall what I wanted to tell him. I was stuttering like a child. Yet that didn't dampen my spirit. Before I could forget why I had come to him in such a state, I spoke with very little cohesion but with enough conviction, "It's about you and Ruby, Arun. I know she is very pretty. It's not your fault, brother. I don't even blame her for that. She is absolutely ok as a classmate. But she doesn't belong to our class. Honestly, she is not the right girl for you. Stay away from her, Yaar. I have spent two long years running after Roma. I couldn't even tell her once. I had my fears. You are a brilliant student, the best in our group. Please, at least, for my sake, stay away from her. She is good, but too good for you. I am your friend, your brother. You mean a lot to me. I am a gone case now. She may not be a bitch. But she is clever and manipulative. She is not for you." I was sobbing. A quarter of cheap whiskey could make anyone emotional, especially when one's emotions are preconceived. He stood up and looked sternly at me. He held my hand and took me to my room. He pushed me to my untidy bed and turned off the light. He didn't say anything. His silence killed me. I cried on my bed and fell asleep. I was too drunk to remember what else I had told him that evening. That night, I skipped my dinner.

A SENSE OF RELIEF

I woke up the next morning, disturbed by the radiance of the morning sun. I felt an instant heaviness in my head. It was due to the hangover, the worst ever I had. I sat on my bed and rubbed my eyes. My roommate was still fast asleep on his bed. I tried to recall what had happened the night before. It was more like peeping into a street side bioscope with a heavily scratched lens through which, one could see blurred vision. I knew I had told something unpleasant to Arun under the spell of alcohol. I desperately wanted to make amends by explaining to him what I meant in a sequence of incoherent utterances. My intention was not to hurt him.

I sipped the morning cup of tea served by the attendant in a hurry and put on my slippers. I quietly came out of my room so as not to disturb my sleeping roommate and made my way towards his room.

He was getting ready to attend a morning lecture. He saw me and smiled at me. To my immense relief, I couldn't notice any sign of anger on his face. He wore a calm expression. "Sorry," I mumbled faintly. He stood quietly there, looking intently at my face. I was not very sure what he was trying to study. Then he held my hands and said, "It's okay, man. I understand your concern and appreciate it. But what was the need to get drunk to tell me this? I know where I stand, and I know my duties and responsibilities. I won't do anything stupid that would jeopardise my career, my ambition, the promises I have made to the people who have brought me here and the dreams I have seen for them. They are the people, who are at the top of my priority list. Ruby is just a friend. Of course, I have some soft corners for her. But it's not love. At least, you should trust me".

I looked at his eyes. They exuded a strong conviction. I felt tremendously relieved. I knew something about his past. I was among a few friends he had, with whom, he had confided some of the painful memories of his shady past. But I still wanted Ruby to stay away from him. I knew how fragile and dangerously destructive human emotions could be. One moment of weakness could put someone's dreams and ambitions at stake. I knew how "inscrutable the ways to a woman's heart are". I knew him. I had seen his tenacity in the past. I sincerely wanted him to survive this critical phase. I placed my palm on my heart and muttered, "All is going to be ok. God is in heaven. All is right with the world."

THE NEXT STEP

I didn't want to give up so soon. I didn't want to work on any presumption. But there was always a lingering sense of doubt that kept haunting me day and night. I wanted to find out what Ruby found so fascinating about Arun. Of course, he was moderately good-looking. But the glamour quotient Ruby carried around her was so grossly incompatible, when one imagined an alliance with Arun, be it physical, social or even intellectual. I decided to develop an acquaintance with Ruby through my friend. On several occasions, whenever I found them together, I tried to barge in with one pretext or another and sat with them. It was difficult to know whether they were happy or unhappy with my intrusion. I couldn't find any change on their faces. Arun was calm and contemplative as he always was, and Ruby was pleasantly polite. Their discussions were mostly related to their academic pursuits. I didn't notice any frivolousness in their behaviour when I was with them. They might be underplaying the symptoms in my presence. However, I noticed one interesting thing. Apart from studies, Ruby was extremely fond of talking about her family members. At times, she presented a larger-than-life image while describing her father, mother, and younger brother. The repetitive nature of this discourse was, to some extent, disgusting to me, as I had never been demonstrative about my feelings for my family. Ruby and her family, Ruby and Arun, Arun and me: I felt like being a tangent of the circle around Ruby and Arun. I was more like the character, who made a special appearance in a negative role in the movie in which they were playing key roles.

But I knew one thing: someone who had an obsessive love for her family would sacrifice anyone, however close or dear they might be, to fulfil her filial obligations, and that was worrying. But I was helpless. I prayed to God to bless my friend with some good sense and protect him from falling into a pit of darkness.

THE GLOW IN THE AUTUMN SKY

There was nothing wrong with a boy befriending a girl. If they sit for a while, they don't become lovers. In our honours group, there was a girl called Saswati. She was smart, frank and kind of tomboyish. But she had a sweet demeanour that everyone around her found so adorable. I met Saswati in our first-ever honours class, taken by Prof. Pattanaik, who was teaching us Shakespeare's *Much Ado About Nothing*. Prof. Pattanaik had that uncanny knack for keeping the class interesting on a hot and humid July afternoon by relating interesting anecdotes from different sources that were relevant to the text he was teaching. Saswati, being a chatterbox, was caught off guard by our teacher while whispering to another girl. The professor severely reprimanded her for interrupting his class. That was when I developed some interest in her for the first time.

But we became friends after an amusing and, at the same time, equally embarrassing incident. Once, all my honours batchmates decided to watch a movie called 'Ardhasatya' at the nearest theatre. The movie had quite an impact on the audience for being extraordinarily different from the stereotypes of the same genre. Saswati had no inhibitions in accompanying us as the lone girl in a group of twenty boys. After our entry into the auditorium, everyone was in a hurry to occupy a seat in the semi-darkness prevailing there. As the movie began, I got so engrossed with the story that I patted the back of the person sitting next to my right to share my excitement. I had done it at least three to four times before the interval. When the lights were turned on for the intermission, I was shocked to see Saswati sitting beside me. It was perhaps the most embarrassing moment of my college life. Without saying a word to her, I left the cinema hall abruptly and came back to my hostel. My stupidity cost me a good night's sleep. The next day I went to meet her to say how sorry I was for the misdemeanour in the Cinema Hall. She had a good laugh at my stupidity and said, "You don't have to be so apologetic about it. I knew it was not intentional. But next time when you go out for a movie, make sure you know who is sitting next to you."

Saswati was not close to me alone. Two of my close friends also shared a wonderful relationship with her. We used to sit in a group, talk, share freshly purchased vegetable cutlets, and drink coffee made by the peon in our department. She was never serious about anything and paid equal attention to everyone. We shared a wonderful chemistry. Saswati's parents knew us. They were not as conservative as most parents in those days. Most importantly, they had trust in their daughter. I was more of a freak, so no one ever took me seriously. I didn't mind that either. The world is a beautiful place as long as you keep living in it with a judicious exercise of your innate goodness. Saswati was one amongst us, who had never crossed the demarcating line between a genuine friend and a possessive, jealous companion. For more than two years, I shared a beautiful chemistry with her.

I wished Ruby had been like Saswati. Ruby was certainly more attractive than Saswati. But there was something inexplicably strange about Ruby. Perhaps, from my limited interactions with her, I had a feeling, vague and undefined though, that she was holding back something within her, maybe a repressed desire, an unfulfilled wish or a troubled psyche. Her polished and polite exterior seemed like a façade, a sly exhibition of something she didn't have, yet frantically craved to flaunt. I found her a bit intimidating, faintly mysterious, like the lines of a poem one could enjoy, while not being able to understand. Ruby could be unpredictable, but Saswati was so transparent.

One unsuccessful, one-sided affair was enough for me to take one more tough call in life. I was certainly not ready to suffer once again from the pangs of unrequited love. I wasn't willing to plunge into that dark pool of love, memory and desire. With Saswati, it was a balanced relationship based on trust and mutual respect and devoid of any expectation that sometimes ruins a healthy relationship between two people. I had never seen any glint in her eyes whenever we met. Her eyes were always calm and serene, like the autumn sky. We didn't even feign to be intellectuals, that we never were.

Saswati had invited me to her home on a couple of occasions. I had met her father, who was a wonderful human being. He had never shown any reservations about accepting me as his daughter's friend, even though I was a boy. Her mother was also loving and caring like all other mothers, but she was not prudish like many of them. They were decent people who would stay away from any complications in life.

I had spent hours with Saswati in cafes, bookshops, the college library and our seminar room. But we were always in a group comprising four boys and two girls. She was the most articulate among the girls. Abinash, one of my honours mates, was a nice guy, reasonably better-looking than me. The girls found him more attractive than many of us. He was from a good family, and his father was a highly successful businessman. Abinash was coming to the college daily in his father's old Lambretta Scooter that he had gifted to his son after he purchased an Ambassador Car. Sometimes, he was seen zooming around the campus, carrying three pillion riders, the last one on the back seat, virtually sitting in a state of suspension. That was fun for all of us as we loved taking a bit of risk in life. For a long time, I doubted that Saswati had a crush on Abinash. I had never tried to verify till we took the examination and left the campus of our dreams for good. I had always been fond of her but never been possessive about her. I had often asked myself, "Can she ever fall in love with me? Am I in love with her?" I had never found an answer. She was just a good friend and, incidentally, a girl. That was how I always treated her.

Unfortunately, I couldn't keep in touch with her when I was at the university. Those were the loneliest days of my life. I had to spend them with a nagging sense of guilt and loss. I felt like the survivor of a shipwreck in the absence of Arun, Vikash, Abinash, Akash, Raju, and a few of my intimate friends from East Hostel, who left me all alone to pursue other viable career options. It was not that I couldn't make new friends at my new destination. But the camaraderie was always missing. Life became meaningless, an empty dream in the absence of the people to whom I was so deeply attached. It was the beginning of a new period in my life, the beginning of an illusory end that held no hope. For three long years, I survived the ordeals of leading a life that didn't mean anything to me except living with perpetual guilt, a 'to-be or not-to-be' state of mind, and a lingering introspective inertia. I became a living ghost. It's not that I didn't make friends at the University. But my life was completely overhauled there.

PART-FOUR

RUMMAGING THROUGH THE SHADOWS AND SILHOUETTES

I have been passing through a rough patch of late. Of course, it's nothing compared to what I had gone through in my childhood. The demons of my childhood days sometimes rise out of their graves and keep snarling at me with their sharp teeth and claws. I never try to forget my childhood afflictions, the nagging impoverishment, my father's premature death, and my days in the orphanage. and the final compromise with my fate. I remember them as vividly as one remembers the best book with a few poignant chapters one has read in one's life. I still cling to those memories because I connect with my past through them. They are like the faint glimmer of hope in a late twilight. Those memories, no matter how painful they are, still make me feel nostalgic because I find within them, my mother looking at me with her love-laden eyes and my brother waiting for me in front of the school hostel, holding a bag containing fritters or ladoos in his hand to hand it over to me. As I emerge from my room, I see the concern, love, and excitement in his eyes. I find Dhani Sir standing near the school gate with a loving smile, holding my annual report card in his hand. I see them all and that sustains me and helps me defeat that scary demon trying to destabilise my world. On a dark, moonless night, those memories twinkle like stars. I visualise a road lying ahead of me. I don't know where it leads to, and I don't see the smoothness or the roughness of this road. I am not too sure about my destination. I ask myself, "How long do I have to live with this borrowed happiness?" My sad past was always so comforting than the fake happiness I feel when I am with those who are so much unlike me yet pretend to be like me. Questions swarm around me like angry bees and sting my soul mercilessly. Those questions hit the bounce board of my inner scepticism and return to me unanswered. Rajiv told me, "You know the answer to your question. In fact, you are the answer to your question. Seek, explore within yourself and discover those answers which haunt you now. They are not from your past. They are from the present, the existential dilemma that keeps you in its captivity."

There is something so fascinating about Rajiv, something I envy and the worst part is that he never envies me. Our yesterdays were radically different: my childhood was spent amidst a perennial longing for parental love and care. But I lost them at a very early age. He was a victim of oppressive love and concern that he had always detested. He spent his entire childhood hoping to live a normal life, the children of his age were living, and he was deprived of it. He grew up in a restricted zone under the strict surveillance of his radical father. He became a rebel. Mine was a battle against my destiny, and he was the one, pitted against his authoritarian family. In a sense, both of us spent our respective childhood with a sense of loss and a sense of deprivation. He never hides anything from me, but I never allow him to see my dark, fragmented world, lest that would scare him off.

He is someone I can always trust. I can rest my head on his shoulder to release my pent-up feelings. We share a typical star equilibrium relationship. But I see Rajiv less these days. I know he has distanced himself from me because of my proximity to Ruby. How can I explain to him that, Ruby is just more than a classmate and less than a friend to me? Unfortunately, the defining and dividing line is somewhat blurred. He doesn't take our relationship lightly. I sometimes struggle with words whenever I try to explain to him the equation of my relationship with Ruby. I know, I stand in a twilight zone. But I also know I don't belong to her class. I still do not understand, why Ruby shows so much interest in me. She is certainly not a serious student who is keen to establish intellectual proximity with me. Neither does she share with me all those frivolous stuff that the girls normally indulge in. I have seen a strange ray of light in her eyes whenever she comes to me, and I fail to understand the truth behind the light. The light keeps me happy for a while and leaves me disoriented the rest of the time. Rajiv calls her a dark butterfly. That hurts me. I ask myself a million times every night, "Do I have feelings for her"? I don't get any answer. "Am I betraying myself"? I don't get any answer. I feel trapped and suffocated; a deep sense of listlessness overtakes me and dismantles my belief system. Why do I feel so exasperated? I am certainly not in love with Ruby. I know my priorities; I know the dreams I have to fulfil. I know how far I am from my goal.

If ever I have to choose between Rajiv and Ruby tomorrow, then I will certainly opt for Rajiv. Rajiv has stood beside me whenever I have struggled with my desperation, my frustration, my unhappiness or every other thing, mundane, emotional or spiritual that threatens to break me into pieces. Rajiv is the only person, who has seen the darkness within me and my struggle when the darkness overpowers me. He stands before me as a beacon of light and seeks to diffuse and dispel the clouds of darkness that keep the sky within me covered, the sky that holds the sun, the moon and millions of stars of happiness. I know Rajiv's weaknesses. I know he is an alcoholic, who has built up his own moral theories. But when it comes to protecting a friend, he becomes a saviour.

Rajiv has a certain duality in his character. He is outspoken and aggressive with those he dislikes. I have seen that sudden spurt of anger within him while dealing with people he is not attached to and that frightens me. But when it comes to dealing with the people he loves, he behaves like a lamb. He never retaliates even when his loved ones hurt him with deliberate malice. Where does he get that strength to absorb so much shock is still a mystery to me. Rajiv becomes stoic while dealing with those people and they sometimes take undue advantage of his love for them. His silence is misconstrued to be his weakness. At home, he has never protested against the dominion of his father. Perhaps he releases all his pent-up frustration against the people who barely matter to him, whenever they try to hurt him. On several occasions, I have seen the lamb turning into a tiger; a wounded one and lethal at times, and that frightens me.

CANDID CONFESSION

I still wonder what Ruby wants from me. She loves to sit with me, spend time with me, and listen to me. But she has never tried to use her seductive charm on me. I would be lying if I said that I don't find her physically attractive. I know most of my friends are crazy for her. She is elegantly tall, fair, and lithe with a pair of large, fascinating eyes. While talking to her, I have occasionally stolen glances at her firm, protruding breasts. A woman can feel what a man is staring at. Some feel happy and proud when they feel the probing male eyes on their bodies, and some feel insulted, angry, and defiled. Ruby must have felt my eyes roving over her breasts, imagining their size and softness. But she has never shown any sign of embarrassment. She is mature enough to accept the sexual predilection of a man.

I am not her only friend from the opposite sex. I have seen her hanging out with boys in mocktail lounges or snack corners, and the comfort level she shares with them is amazing. At times, to be honest, I have felt the inevitable sting of jealousy. But it lasts for a short time, leaving me unsettled for a while. I never give up; I think, speculate, and then draw the strength to fill the void with positive thoughts that are, in fact, self-consolations. I still believe I am not in love with Ruby, and neither is she with me. My feelings for her are a quaint admixture of both fascination and admiration, born out of the fancy of a country lad that gradually grows and pervades his entire being, condenses itself into a weird fantasy and sits firmly on the subconscious. It's more of an obsession than love. Ruby is not the girl with whom I can ever fall in love with.

Rajiv is right. She doesn't belong to my league, nor do I belong to her class. But I can't ignore her. I wait for her every day in the seminar library, prepare at night what I would share with her the day after, even though they are mostly the boring academic stuff, and feel a strange nervous restlessness within myself if she gets late, sometimes biting my nails, shaking my legs, wringing my fingers. But again, I don't call it love. But if that is not love, then what is love? We meet in light to explore each other's darkness, and I draw strength from that. Is she the tunnel or the light at the end of it? Rajiv blames Ruby, calls her a seductress, and warns me to stay away from her. But I feel otherwise. Ruby may be a psychological manifestation of my desire to transcend the reality that surrounds me, suffocates me, and drives me to nothingness. Through her, I may be seeking gratification from my unfulfilled desires, which I know are unattainable.

Rajiv does not accept my interpretation because he has never borne in his heart the traumas and tribulations someone experiences for being neglected, ignored and pushed into the darkness that perpetuates a feeling of one's rootlessness. He does not understand the anguish of being tagged as a subaltern. He has never lived in two different worlds, one that loves him but disowns him and the other that accepts him but is never accepted by him. He is still miles away from fulfilling the expectations of people who are his own yet not his own. He doesn't have to depend on someone's generosity to fulfil his dreams. He stands miles away from my inner chaos. He always thinks about people who are close to him and goes out of his way to help them. I distinctly remember that, when I was suffering from viral fever, he spent nearly three days sitting beside my bed, recording my temperature, taking care of my medicines and diet, and the examination was just a month away. I know I can't be like Rajiv. I can't be complacent like him. My topmost priority has to be my career and my family. Rajiv can either love or hate, accept or reject people. Rajiv has not seen life in a twilight zone. He has never seen his distorted image in a convex mirror and shrieked with horror. He might have seen demons in his nightmares but never fought with them. Rajiv doesn't know how dreams crumble, and desires die when they are baked by poverty. He has never walked barefoot on a street on fire. I have always appreciated his concern, but I feel disappointed because my best friend doesn't understand my predicament.

DATING MY DESTINY

I got an invite from Ruby today to visit the famous snack bar at College Square. Normally, we stay away from this place. It's a place where the children of the elites throng around for fun. We do not belong to their class. I have seen the snack bar from a distance. I have seen smart boys and girls flocking together, rubbing their shoulders, completely oblivious of the judgmental glare of society and the values they might have learnt from their parents and grandparents at home. Snacks Bar is a place that provides a safe rendezvous for the rich, carefree, uninhibited youngsters, eager to enjoy every drop of happiness in life. With its glamour and brand value, the Snacks Bar is the secret gateway to enjoying everything that is forbidden and seemingly clandestine. After all, we all love to imitate the rich.

Initially, I was reluctant to accompany Ruby to a place I did not belong to. I know, the place is a shade expensive. But I get enough money from two government-sponsored scholarships to afford a little bit of luxury occasionally. Snack Bar is the ultimate fantasy of lower-middle-class and poor students. I do not have the courage to share the update with Rajiv. I do not have an iota of doubt about his reaction. But I don't want to disappoint Ruby either.

I know Ruby's friends will be there, those rich, spoilt brats. But I have to give them a cold shoulder and get the feel of the hype that goes with this place. They won't take my presence kindly there. I may be snubbed, bullied and treated with a degree of shocking hostility. But I always believe that class is just a social construct. They all know my superiority but are too jealous to acknowledge it. I feel an overwhelming urge to break the stigma that surrounds me and celebrate life the way they do. It's less about going out with Ruby and more about dating my destiny. I think this is the right time to assert myself and let those boys know who I am. It's the right time to come out of the shadow of self-negation, which has been hounding my existence all these years.

ARUN AND SASWATI

One night, I found Arun sitting on the hostel rooftop, his eyes fixed on the night sky. Was he counting the stars? Was he looking at the moon or waiting for a shooting star to make a wish (people say those wishes are fulfilled one day)? I walked up to him quietly and placed my hand on his shoulder. He was startled and looked at me with a glint of surprise in his eyes. He was certainly not expecting me. I wasn't sure whether he was happy with my abrupt appearance or angry. His face betrayed no emotion. He just asked me quietly,

"How do you know I would be here?" "It's just a gut feeling, man. You love to be alone when you need time to think of yourself and the suffering humanity; this is the best place to sit and think and find an answer to the question that perplexes you. I have known you for three years. We almost grew up under one roof during these years". He was like a protagonist of one of Dostoevsky's novels to me. He listened to me silently and spoke, "Yes, we grew up not under one roof, but under one shade like a flock of lambs for years", he said, not trying to hide his sarcasm. "Whenever we have tried to bleat, we have been punished. Just think of our expulsion from the East Hostel; recall the indignant expression of our English teacher when I tried to contest his interpretation in a general class. We are here to listen to people, listen to all those bull shits that muddle up our minds. In the evening, a few fucking assholes come to our hostel in a group to invade our privacy, destroy the sanctity of this hostel, and the best we can do is to bleat like lambs".

He was perceptibly angry and, therefore, fuming like an angry but exasperated individual. I didn't know the cause of his anger. Nonetheless, I wanted to placate him, to blow out the fire within him. I held his hand and said, "Look, things are not as bad as they seem to be. I know we have been wronged in one way or another, sometimes disproportionately too. But we are not the first, nor even the last, to be at the receiving end of an unjust system. There are many who lead a dog's life. We are always a shade better off with our small shares of happiness, enjoyment, and entitlement." He was still quite upset. I knew something might have hurt him deeply. I had never seen him raving and ranting about something. I sat near him with my hand on his shoulder and looked at the sky with its autumnal glory. The occasional gust of wind brushed against my bare skin. I kept counting the twinkling stars silently.

Honestly speaking, life had been, at times, unkind but not so harsh to me. After leaving home, I hardly complained against life. During those three years, I had tried hard to forget my unhappy childhood. Perhaps the sense of freedom had made me more empathetic. Many a time, I tried to place myself in my father's position and ask myself the question that tortured me: "How would I have behaved had I been in his position?"

GIVING SPACE

I started meeting Saswati frequently. Sitting in a nearby coffee shop quite frequently, we used to chat for at least an hour. She paid the bill without grumbling, for she knew, I couldn't afford to treat her with coffee. With whatever I used to get from my parents as pocket money, it was invariably difficult for me to clear the monthly credit I owed to the tea shop owner, though he had never embarrassed me by asking for money before the first week of every month. For him, at least, I was not a defaulter. Saswati knew, with the meagre amount I used to get from home and the bad habits I had fallen into, I turned into a pauper after the first fifteen days of the month, waiting for windfall gains to manage the next fifteen days. This is the usual story of every spendthrift.

To be honest, I didn't always relish Saswati's generosity. Most of the time, she had to be extra generous by extending her hospitality to a few shameless friends of mine, who never declined her invitation, even out of courtesy. Saying no to her had always been difficult for me. She was the only girl who was my friend.

Arun never joined us, though Saswati had invited him a couple of times to the coffee shop. I had never forced him to. We respected each other's sentiments and self-respect. Saswati was aware of that too, and never went out of the way to invite Arun with an insistence that he would have found embarrassing. In the coffee shop, we sometimes discussed Arun, the incomprehensible and formidable part of his personality, his intellectual exuberance that we all found so attractive, the mystic look on his face and his reclusive temperament. We discussed his affiliation with Ruby too. Saswati didn't like Ruby, and the reasons were not far to seek. Ruby didn't belong to our world. Saswati had expressed her apprehension about the future of that never-to-be-formed alliance. But each time she raised the topic, I always tried to evade it.

I, at times, seriously asked myself, "Can I ever fall in love with Saswati"? But I was sure that, after all serious introspection, I would get a negative answer. It was not that, I didn't get attracted to girls; I had one unreciprocated love affair in my account, and Saswati was reasonably pretty, though she lacked Ruby's vivacity. After the cinema hall debacle, I found a friend in her, a friend who could understand me, who was critical of me, but appreciated my frankness and accepted me as what I was, not as what she wanted me to be. I never got tempted to spoil such a beautiful relationship with expectations. At times, my friends teased me about Saswati. Once, Vikash told me, "Don't you know she is in love with you? Have you never noticed the blush on her cheeks while she talks to you? How can you be so naïve, Yaar? She looks visibly happy when you are around. She is just downplaying her emotions. She knows how unpredictable you are, and that's why she never makes any advances". I just shrugged it off. Not that I didn't relish what Vikash said. But I lacked the courage to look at Saswati's face and see her reactions when she was with me. "Love to me is a premature foetus that gets aborted a few days after it is conceived." I was happy with the idea of being with a girl like Saswati. Friendship with her was a bonus to me and I didn't want to stretch it further to be disappointed once again. I couldn't think of a failed relationship with her. I killed the discussion then and there.

Arun also liked Saswati, although he had maintained an ostensible distance from her. He was fiercely possessive about me and critical of my relationship with my friends but never said a line when he found me sitting with Saswati. I knew he didn't trust me, but perhaps he trusted Saswati and lived with the hope that I might change myself to become a more practical person, and she would be instrumental in bringing about that miraculous change, a hope, I was sure, would never be fulfilled. I had made up my mind during the first year on that campus that, I would never do anything, that the so-called good boys were there to achieve. I shed my old skin to grow a new one. So, that was the only transformation I went through after waiting for it for sixteen long years, and I wouldn't let it go so easily. And Saswati had never been preachy or authoritative in her behaviour with me. She always respected my way of looking at things, never imposed her ideas on me and never interfered with what I did, though she didn't appreciate them all. That was what Arun liked about Saswati, and that was why, he never resented my friendship with her.

A SEALED BOX AND A MAGIC WAND

I feel an unusual surge of nostalgia these days. It's more like the silent waves of the evening sea. It's a feeling rising out of my alienation, the recent discovery of my sense of rootlessness, the disturbing feeling of me not being me, and an obsessive desire to belong to a place that would accept me unconditionally. I know I don't belong to this place, the people here. But where do I belong to? Not to my home, to my family members and neither to the people who claim they own me. I remember the story of King Hariścandra of the Ikṣvākus, who was required to sacrifice his son Rohita to Varuṇa, the god of ocean and water. The king couldn't think of sacrificing his dearest child to save his cursed province from the horrific spell of famine. A Brahmin boy named Śunaḥśepa was substituted for Rohita, but before the completion of the ritual, lord Varuna took pity on the helpless, poor Brahmin boy who was later adopted by Viśvāmitra. I read this story in Chnadamama during my pre-university days. Rajiv had a huge collection of them and he brought them from his home in his aluminium trunk.

Rajiv is never miserly when it comes to sharing. He is the only person I can confide with. But I still have some secrets that I have never shared with him. May be as friends, we are still evolving. Rajiv doesn't hide things from me. At times, he is shockingly candid, and that is what I admire about him. But I can't be like him. His past is like a simple story punctuated by sadness and happiness. But mine is a journey through the purgatorial fire. The light in my life has been blinded by darkness. So, crying all alone has been a cathartic release for me.

Rajiv must have noticed a change within me. I have seen the shadow of worry on his face. But he doesn't know what exactly is wrong with me. He is not the kind of guy who gives up so soon. But he always prefers a balanced relationship with me, devoid of selfish expectations, based on trust, love and care. It's not the usual give-and-take relationship. The space we allow each other holds this relationship like glue between two youngsters having plenty of reasons to be jealous of each other, fight with each other and be insecure about each other. But that never happens. Of late I have noticed a change in Rajiv. He has spent time with me regularly for the last two weeks. Perhaps he is vaguely expecting that, I will open up one day, and he will set everything right by waving his magic wand. But does he have one?

Rajiv does not know anything about my predicament, and I don't want to share anything with him right now because that will disturb him. He has neglected his studies during the last two years. He has started preparing for the final examination seriously for the first time. He is a bright student, but he doesn't take anything seriously. It's his rebellion against his father. All these years, he has tried to prove him wrong. It's not that he doesn't love him. It's all about the clash of ideology between a father and a son. I, of course, don't understand much because I lost my father when I was three years old. But I know one thing: Rajiv is playing a dangerous game with his own life, in his attempt to prove his father wrong.

THE KALEIDOSCOPE OF EMOTIONS

It was Holi. Right from the morning, my friends started coming in small groups with Gulal and water solvent colours in hand. I had kept my door closed after sipping my morning tea. I was allergic to the smell of Gulal. During my childhood, I was not allowed to play Holi with the boys my age, because over-exposure to colours and prolonged hours of bathing in the river could trigger flu followed by fever. I had always tried to defy all the restrictions imposed by my father, save the one involving Holi because I never liked the smell and the feel of Gulal. But that was my last year. I was a bit indecisive, as it could be my last chance to play Holi with my friends. When they started banging on my door with the aggressive severity of a group of soldiers attacking a small province, I had to open my door before it gave way. There they were, a group of ten to twelve friends, their faces disfigured with colours. They pounced upon me like hungry predators and smeared colours all over my body. It was a predetermined attack to leave a memorable imprint of the celebration on someone, who had hated its smell throughout his life. They didn't even spare the undergarments. For a while, I felt angry, insulted and defiled. But friendship is always about putting up with the pranks of your friends. There should not be any room for any grudge or grumble. I lay on the floor of the corridor, allowing this bizarre invasion of my privacy by my friends. To be honest, to my horror, I found I was enjoying this onslaught.

I played Holi throughout the day, roamed around the campus like a painted devil, and stopped near the ladies' hostel to wish the girls a Happy Holi. Some of them threw Gulals through their windows from the second and third floors. We could get a glimpse of their disfigured faces from their windows. They looked sad and jealous on seeing us roaming around the campus without any inhibition. For a while, I felt sad for them. They seemed like damsels in distress, imprisoned in an enchanted castle by a demon. I remembered all those fascinating fairy tales, I had gone through during my childhood, when I had no other pastime to follow. I came back to the hostel nearly at 3 p.m., feeling happy but exhausted. I had a late lunch and slept like a log till evening.

When I woke up, it was already dark. The borders were creating a lot of commotion outside. Some of them were drunk, and some had taken bhang Coolfi from College Square. I suddenly remembered that I had not met Arun the whole day. It was something abnormal because we used to meet each other at least once before going to college. On holidays, we used to spend at least one hour together. How could I afford to forget him throughout the day? How could I forget to make him a part of my maiden Holi celebration? How could I be so selfishly obsessed with my happiness?

I went to his room. He was perhaps asleep, as there was no light coming from his room. It came as a kind of surprise for me, as he normally studied during that time. I knocked on his door gently, once, twice, then thrice and for the fourth time. I started getting worried when I got no response. I knocked on the door harder. After a while, to my immense relief, I heard someone's footsteps. He opened the door. His eyes were swollen. Something was disturbing about his appearance. He didn't look like someone who had woken up from a deep sleep; rather, he looked sad and lonely. I had to apologise to him for not being able to meet him in the morning. He didn't say anything.

He just asked me to sit on the chair near his bed. I discovered a pack of Gold Flake cigarettes on his table for the first time. I asked him, "When did you start smoking?" He retorted on an aggressive note, "The day you started drinking". I knew he was lying. His lies did not hurt me, nor did his aggression. I was used to his change of mood during those three to four years. Such unpredictable behaviour is a part of human psychology during adolescence. All of us were trying to cope with the hormonal changes and the probability of profuse secretion of testosterone in our bodies. He sat on his bed silently. He looked pale and drained out. But I had lost the courage to ask him the reason. I asked him to watch a movie with me, but he gently declined with the pretext that, he had to prepare a few urgent notes. I didn't insist. I knew something was wrong somewhere. I had never asked him about Ruby for some time. I had not seen him sitting with her anywhere on the campus.

I came back to my room and sat gloomily on my bed. My roommate had gone home to celebrate Holi. I was feeling concerned for Arun. For the first time during all those three-plus years, I could sense a negativity within him. I had always wanted him to do well in life and fulfil his mother's and his mentor's dreams. "Is he losing his ways?" I asked myself. But I didn't want the day to end with such a disappointing note. I brought out a half-empty pint of Old Monk from my shelf, poured one large peg into a steel glass, mixed some water with it and drank it down in a hurry. I felt my throat burning, and later, it started burning my inside. I felt a fire in my head. I forgot Arun and his gloom. The night was spent like a reverie.

THE SHRINKING UNIVERSE

I don't feel like meeting people these days. As it is, I never waste time like Rajiv, hanging out with a bunch of good-for-nothing friends. Those exhausting rounds of exciting amusements certainly do not suit me. It's not that I am a reclusive idiot who doesn't like the vibrant world around me. But life has taught me a few nasty lessons in a hard way to be pragmatic. I sometimes feel jealous of Rajiv for the way in which he treats life so lightly. But I can't do that. I still search for my identity in that basket full of fritters Babu Bhai carries every morning to school. I still see myself sitting with Babu Bhai under the shade of a mango tree, waiting for school boys to come during recess and buy the fritters in a hurry. At night, I clutch a handful of my bedsheet, mistaking it to be a part of my mother's saree. In the stillness of the night, I search for that lonely child who had lost his father even before he could know what a father's love was all about. I search for the child who was forcibly deported to an orphanage to save him from starvation. Being reclusive was not an option for me; it was a compulsion, deeply psychological.

I know it's Holi today. My friends are celebrating outside. I hear Rajiv's voice. It sounds euphoric. Perhaps he is doing it for the first time in his life. I have heard from him how he was forced to languish in unhappiness, pining for a little bit of freedom, which his friends had in abundance. He had a painful past. But my past was a journey through darkness in quest of light that kept deceiving me. I have never compared myself with Rajiv. I love him with all his faults and frailties. I have never been so fond of anyone else with the same intensity ever in my life. He has a mind of his own and a beautiful heart. He feels, thinks, and empathises; that's why he is so endearing.

I felt bad for being so rude to Rajiv. Why should I use him as a receptacle of my frustration? Why should I allow him to witness the battle being fought within me every moment, the battle I am mentally getting ready to lose, yet go ahead with my vanquished ego? I have to speak to Rajiv before it's too late. I owe him an apology.

THE WALL

"What clicks in this world, makes life easier and worth living? It's either half-truth or half-lie because both truth and lie suck the life out of us. You have to make your own compound of truth and lie to live in a world, that predominantly remains opaque. The truth kills you every time you accept it, and the lie grows within you like a malignant tumour, spreading rapidly to every part of your body, making death slow but excruciatingly painful. Half truth or half lie is more like a medicine that deceives your system into thinking that all is well".

I didn't want Arun to die with the truth, nor did I want him to live with a lie. I knew he was running after a mirage. How sincerely I wished to stop him. But I failed. I lacked the courage to be truthful. I badly wanted a concoction of truth and lie to break the lethal part of his illusion while keeping the less harmful part intact, and I found none.

He apologised to me the next day. I was in a state of intoxication. How did I respond? Did I hurt him in an inebriated state? Even though he was hiding from me, I was sure, something had gone terribly wrong between him and Ruby, and he was silently suffering for that. I knew he didn't want to be ridiculed by a few insensitive friends, and neither did he want to become a part of the gossip, especially when it involved someone like Ruby. He was fighting a war within himself, one that had ripped his soul apart, shaken his conviction, and hurled him to the bottom of a dark dungeon. The hope of being rescued looked bleak.

Dealing with someone's trauma with empathy and understanding is always tough, as we are all vulnerable to our own prejudices that we place over everything else. Moreover, winning the trust of the victim, whose cooperation would make your job easier, is way tougher than it seems to be. It's more like getting an inner view of a dark room through a crack on the wall.

I should have talked to Ruby and asked her what went wrong between them. At least I should have talked to one of her close friends to get to the bottom of the trouble. I knew quite a few of them. I didn't know what to do. I felt terribly confused. A wall stood between me and Arun, alienating me from him. I saw Arun encased in a trunk, floating on the deep sea and I, standing on the shore forlorn, dejected, betrayed and devastated. No matter how deeply I was attached to Arun, I was not his saviour. The feeling of despondency kept rattling me every time I thought of Arun and his existential crisis.

IN LOVE WITH THE CLOUDS

I don't find clouds in the sky these days. Every year, they go home for a break as the monsoon retreats, leaving a faint trail of their temporal existence on the opaque winter sky. I wait for the clouds like the cursed Tantalus. With the onset of summer, I feel an inexplicable restlessness in my heart. I hear an indistinct blowing of the conch somewhere from one far end of the sky. My mother used to tell me fascinating stories about the abode of clouds, how they come and how they go. She used to tell me stories about their reluctant mother, bidding them a 'not so happy farewell' as they got ready every year to sail back to the sky.

I fell in love with the clouds when I was a child. The stories about the clouds were more enticing to me than fairy tales. I was never afraid of them, no matter how dark they were or how sinister they appeared to be. I was as much in love with those dark, pot-bellied clouds as I was with those bright but scary streaks of lightning. Clouds were the damsels in distress, and I was their gallant prince, vowing to protect them from the gusty wind or the glaring sun. It was a very long story of disappointment and heartbreak. I could neither save them nor keep them with me. From a cloud lover, I became a cloud watcher.

I grew up with sun, rain, and winter. As a child, I found nature incredibly attractive, especially that part of nature that always remains dark, luxuriant, and unexplored. I find a reflection of nature within me as if we have grown together under one roof as twin brothers, our love and interdependence intertwined like tangled creepers. From nature, I have learnt love, spontaneity, and acceptance. Nature is so much like poetry that one reads, understands and appreciates. The lines unknowingly become yours and you start using them whenever you feel like letting out your emotions without being stifled by any inhibition. Nature is an extension of myself.

Ruby is so much unlike me. She is soft-spoken, polished, and careful about her etiquette, a sharp contrast to the uncouth country lads like me and my friends. We speak from our heart, open our minds without inhibitions, fall and flounder, but never learn to rectify ourselves. But Ruby weighs twice before she speaks to someone. She thinks multiple times before she speaks a line even to the friends with whom she hangs out throughout the day. Those boys are spoilt children of stinkingly rich fathers. The air of superiority and arrogance becomes so apparent in their appearance. They can't accept a simple village lad with so many behavioural imperfections as their friend. Ruby shouldn't have invited me to the snack bar that day. Standing isolated in one corner and watching Ruby and her friends having fun was so humiliating.

Why did Ruby invite me to a group when she knew well that, I would have serious adjustment issues? Did she do it deliberately? Did she want to prove to me that being a good student is not everything in life? You have to be complete in every respect to be successful in life. Sitting on the parapet with my legs hanging, I looked at the clouds in the sky. They were changing their shape and colour every two minutes. They were all in a hurry to reach their destination. I saw a faint outline resembling Ruby on a cloud floating in the evening sky. Was she sneering at my stupidity? I stood up. The sky put on an eerie glow, just like a scowling face. I have committed a blunder, and I must make amends. I got up and ran to my room.

THE MOON, THE VENUS AND FALLING IN LOVE

Love is the biggest deception in life. Love kills you every moment, kills you with hope that is never going to be fulfilled, and kills you with dreams that are never going to be realised. Love kills you yet drags you away from death. That's the biggest paradox in the life of someone in love. One of my cousins was madly in love with a girl from our neighbourhood. Life was like a dream to him. But one day, he learned that the girl was getting married to an engineer. He was devastated. That was his final year. He tried his best to meet the girl, to convince her parents. But the irony was that the girl refused to meet him. The prospect of marrying a well-established engineer looked more promising to her than bracing for the uncertainty of being in love with someone who might not be able to say what shape his 'tomorrow' would take. The girl got married after a few days and lived happily ever after. My cousin dropped his examination and slipped into a state of depression. For him, it was more like experiencing death in life. Love nearly killed him while keeping him alive to realise what an existence called life in death could really mean.

I was very close to experiencing that old familiar fear. Arun was not someone like me who never cared to discover the subtle differences in love, infatuation, fling or crush. I barely took a month to come out of the frustration. But Arun was never so casual like me. I didn't want him to experience that terrible feeling of being used and then dumped. I didn't want to see his dreams crumbling down like a house of cards; I didn't want to see his world getting fragmented with the tremor of deception in love, leaving a crater in his heart.

No matter how effectively he tried to hide it, I knew he was in love with Ruby and the truth was that a girl like Ruby could never fall in love with a boy like Arun. Something had gone wrong between both of them which Arun didn't want to share with me. He was too proud to admit that Ruby was a mistake in his life, and I was so afraid to probe into his private life.

I had once studied his palm, though I was an amateur palmist. I had read a few good books on palmistry when I was a schoolboy. My father was a reputed astrologer who had given me a few tips on palm reading. There was a break in Arun's heart line while the segment after the break was inclined towards the lunar mount, ending with a cross. Both the lunar mount and the mount of Venus were so prominent on his palms. One inspires your creative urge, while the other indicates your passion. I had warned him of heartbreak once while reading his hands casually. I had every reason to feel concerned about Arun's love life in future.

THE UNEXPLORED OCEAN

Rajiv never talks about his friendship with Saswati, although I know he likes her. I have never had any feeling that she is more than a friend to Rajiv. They share a wonderful chemistry, but I have never heard anyone discussing their proximity. May be, it's due to Rajiv's projected lack of seriousness in life. To everyone, Rajiv is what he is: an open book. But I always have my doubts about that, even though I know, how he overcame his unreciprocated infatuation for one of our classmates. I have queer feelings about Rajiv being in love with someone, the mystery girl. I think he is still not ready to disclose her name to me or to any of his close friends. But I have seen it in his eyes, that feeling of being lost, and read it on his face, which normally betrays no other emotion than that of a distant happiness one feels like the faint aroma of unknown flowers blooming in the wilderness.

Rajiv writes wonderful poems, that are mostly pessimistic in sharp contrast to his character. The themes of most of his poems are death, decay and betrayal. They are mostly dark with an intense yearning to quit this world that offers nothing to someone who loves to lead a simple and unostentatious life. One can't write such beautiful, sad poems if he is not suffering within himself, something he is afraid of sharing with others for fear of being misunderstood or not being properly reciprocated. Rajiv is passionate about everything and everyone, including his friends and his surroundings. Rajiv rarely writes about love. Perhaps he is trying to hide his love somewhere at the bottom of an unknown ocean where there is no wave, no ripple, no palpable movement of any sort.

I have never tried to be inquisitive about his private life, the secrets, if he has any, and his dreams because Rajiv is not seemingly an introvert like me. At times, he is shockingly candid, and the very next moment, he gets quiet like the sky at dawn. The degree of unpredictability in his behaviour makes him more attractive as a friend. I sometimes feel Rajiv's compassion outweighs his love for me, and that makes me feel miserable. Unlike other friends, he certainly does not find my intellectual superiority 'the piece de resistance of my character'. He never solicits my guidance in studies like most of my friends do because, that is one thing that has never been one of the priorities of his life. I find his anti-intellectual stand a bit intriguing. I know he has a mind of his own. He thinks like an intellectual, exploring an order in chaos, a preexisting order in anarchy that he always talks about. I don't call it duplicity in his character. It may be a deep understanding of things that we consider delusional. He knows I know him better than others, and he doesn't appreciate the idea of opening up everything before me, though I am his best friend. He enjoys keeping a tiny part of himself wrapped in darkness like that mystery girl in his life.

AIR BUBBLES

Ruby invited me to a private party hosted by one of her friends. I knew this would happen. I politely declined the invitation. I didn't mean to hurt her. But I didn't want to play this hide-and-seek game with her. That sucks the life out of me. I told her, "See, I don't belong to your league.

I can't pretend to be friendly with a group of self-styled neo-liberals with scant respect for the ethics and values we have been born and brought up with. Your friends consider me Stone Age primitive. I have seen that cold contempt, a feeling of rejection in their eyes. It is so apparent in their behaviour. They are downplaying that feeling of rejection just because you put pressure on them and force them to accept me for reasons best known to you. But I am tired of being treated as a lab rat".

Ruby was not expecting such a blunt denial from me. She looked at me in shocked disbelief. For a moment, she was livid with anger. Perhaps she was never used to hearing 'no' from someone she had been close with. But after a while, she cooled down a little bit and said, "Don't behave like a prudish pig, man. These guys are also your friends. It's another thing, you don't like them. But I have always shielded you from any kind of hostility from my friends." I said, "Look, Ruby, I have got nothing against your friends. But I am not like them. I struggle with adjustment issues whenever I am with them. I have issues with my coping mechanism. You have always been very caring or rather protective about me. I am really grateful to you. But we normally protect someone, who is weak and insecure, and I am neither of the two. I feel perfectly ok with my friends. But I am sorry to say, every time I sit with you, the pride of me being me gets shattered. I know, and you know that too, we belong to two separate worlds. I have accepted you as a friend for reasons unknown to me. I am still struggling to figure out why I cherish your company and feel happy when you are with me. Why have I overlooked the compatibility issues with you, whereas I fail to do the same when I am with your friends? I am so confused about my feelings for you. I am sorry, dear, but it's all botched up. It's more like solving a difficult equation and getting the first few steps wrong."

Ruby gave me a cold stare, and it was evident that she was not happy with my impassioned confession. Then she spoke to me with a cold but honest tone, "Arun, I have always appreciated you or rather respected you for being a good human being and an exceptionally brilliant student. Yes, I like you too, and that's why I invited you to hang out with my friends. Right from the beginning, I did not want this relationship to be misunderstood as anything beyond a healthy relationship between two classmates. Listening to you has been a pleasure, and learning from you has been a privilege. But you misunderstood me and misinterpreted this relationship. I am sorry for being the cause of any form of emotional turmoil you have been passing through, and most importantly, to be very honest with you, my friends have all along been the top priorities in my life. It may sound crazy, but if I can choose between my blood relatives and friends, I would gladly go for the latter. I treat all my friends almost with equal love and care. No one is more important than the other. This so-called egalitarian feeling is deep in the gut. I have never faked it". She took a long breath and started again, "You know, I have grown up with them, spent those lovely days at school, and shared the troubled moments of a confused adolescent with them. My only regret is that you pulled yourself away when I was getting ready to accept you as one among them. Now I realise, you were never there in my core group; you never tried to be there. All these days, you have been nursing your wounded ego in seclusion. I was so wrong, so stupidly wrong! Anyways, it's absolutely okay. Live your own life with your friends. Let me live with my delusions. You are right: we belong to two different worlds that can never merge. Live happily in your lovely, little, self-contained world and let me go back to my own fucking world, my bunch of friends whom you treat as bragging assholes. But they are what they are, and I am what I am. So are you, too." She spun like a wheel and left the place in a hurry. I was reeling under the impact of the spontaneity of her outburst, the melodramatic articulation of her impression of me, and the volley of swear words she used for the first time in my presence, though they are so commonly used by her friends. I sat there on the wooden bench in the history honours classroom, staring at the thin ray of light coming through one of the broken ventilators of that room. But that was not enough to dispel the darkness within me. I stood up and spoke loudly, "Fuck off, just fuck off. I don't have any regret in calling your friends fucking assholes, though I have never used those filthy words that you people use so frequently" I felt incredibly relieved, just like having a huge orgasm after the first ever masturbation of my early adolescent days. It was very close to that ultimate feeling of winning over your repressed libido. Did I disobey God? Did I break any taboo of the society that's mine and will always remain mine? I saw multiple answers to my question floating in eternity like air bubbles. It's six o'clock, time to get back to my hostel.

THE DANCE OF DEATH

It was mid-April. The final examination was just a few days away. Most of us had temporarily said goodbye to our frivolous lifestyle and got back to our studies to make up for what we had lost for neglecting our studies during the last two years so badly. It was more like patching up holes in a sinking ship. There were tell-tale signs of desperation on everyone's face. No more nocturnal visits to the railway station for midnight snacking, no more loitering in front of the lady's hostel to tease the sweet, soft, elegant inmates. From morning till midnight, it was just about studying and surviving the self-inflicted pain of reducing our quota of sleep at night. It was a do-or-die situation for all of us, the last part of the battle, that someone like me was never going to win.

I barely got any chance to meet Arun. He had separated himself from most of us. It was his last chance to fulfil his dream, the dream that his teacher had seen for him the day he became the school topper. It was his last chance to prepare for the most decisive test of his life: the most challenging JNU Entrance. If you managed to get a berth there, you were halfway through your journey to crack civil services. At least, that was the story told to us by our ambitious and successful seniors. I had never tried to know the veracity of this hypothesis. I was neither ambitious nor bright like Arun. For me, it was just a journey all along, from repression to emancipation. I simply wanted to get a seat in one of the universities in Odisha. I didn't want to disappoint my father. I knew he did not have very high expectations from me. I had prayed more fervently for Arun's success than for my own. Though it sounds incredibly stupid, it was the truth.

It was the 15th of April, just a day after Visubha Sankranti. We were all quietly studying in our rooms in the evening. Suddenly, we heard a hullabaloo that gradually got louder and louder. Most of us ran to the ground floor, keeping our doors ajar. What we heard was a bolt from the blue. One of the senior boys from the P.G. Wing of our hostel, Prakash Bhai had fallen off the rooftop of the hostel for the Post Graduate Students. Hearing an unusual thud, some of his friends rushed to the inner quadrangle to find him, to their horror, lying in a pool of blood. The rear part of the skull was almost smashed, and blood was gushing out from the injury as his lifeless body lay on the ground. All of us stood horrified, watching the gruesome spectacle in total disbelief. Prakash Bhai was not just an ordinary student staying in our hostel. He was a youth icon. We used to love him. There were innumerable instances of Prakash Bhai going the extra mile to help a poor student in need. He had often fought with the manager of the hostel mess for serving us substandard food. He had even arranged an extra TV for us so that, we could watch the cricket matches when no empty chairs were available in the common room. His sudden death in such a mysterious situation left us stunned.

His cremation took place in the presence of his family members after the autopsy report was received by the hostel superintendent. The doctor who conducted the postmortem had found traces of bhang in his stomach. But taking Bhang was never so unnatural for any of us. At least 33% of the inmates had the habit of taking Bhang every evening. We had heard that, he had a break-off with his girlfriend recently, and to forget the trauma, he had increased his daily intake of Bhanga. Perhaps he fell from the roof in a state of intoxication. The poor girl was staying in the girl's hostel, and a group of senior boys went to her hostel, angry and drunk and threatened the watchman to open the hostel gate or call the girl downstairs. The scared watchman called the police after consulting the warden. The local IIC, after his arrival, did a commendable job as he pacified the angry mob using an ingenious cocktail of sympathy, grief, flattery and to top them all veiled threats. The boys dispersed that night with a vow to come again the next day to settle the score with the girl. The girl left the hostel the very next day early in the morning and didn't come back to take her final examination. Thus ended a tragic story of a man, who, within his short span of life, had endeared himself to everyone in his surroundings. A life was lost, and someone's career was ruined. Were they the consequences of falling in love?

THE MYSTERY CONTINUES

A few days after the tragic death of Prakash Bhai, when we were trying to recuperate from the shock, another post-grad student from the same hostel fell off the roof and landed dead almost on the same spot, where the body of Prakash Bhai was found. The news spread like wildfire on the campus. The victim was not so popular among the inmates like Prakash Bhai. He was a final-year student of the philosophy department, an unassuming young man with nothing to boast of. But two consecutive deaths within such a short span was no less intriguing than the story of a suspense movie. Moreover, it couldn't be just a coincidence that the bodies were found on one spot with identical head injuries. When the entire campus was reeling under the fear of paranormal activities in the P.G Hostel, speculations were rife among the students that these two deaths could be cold-blooded murders by a mysterious psychopath, and the perpetrator was moving still at large. After the second death, the city police took the matter seriously and an Additional S.P. from the crime branch department was given the charge of investigating the angle of homicide or murder. Many students from the same hostel, as well as a few postgraduate students from our hostel, were dragged to the police station for interrogation. It was a daunting task for the city police to establish a plausible motive behind the murder because none of the victims had any apparent enemies, and both of them were staying away from college politics or any other controversies. To the best of everyone's knowledge, no girl was involved in the second case. A state of panic prevailed on the campus. With the onset of the evening, the hostel boarders preferred to stay indoors. The hostel rooftops, which used to bustle with the commotions created by the boarders on summer days, wore a deserted look. The boarders who had been allocated single rooms in recognition of their academic excellence invited their friends, who were staying in four seated rooms, to sleep with them at night.

The P.G. Hostel became a huge haunted mansion like those seen in horror movies, where the inmates were living with a perpetual fear of being the victim of one more catastrophe. The mysterious appearance of the shadowy figure on the hostel rooftop night after night became a recurring topic among the students in the nearby tea stalls. However, as per the available reports, only a very few boarders had seen the dark silhouette at night. The staircase leading to the rooftop was permanently closed and sealed by the hostel warden. The boarders spent sleepless nights amidst the worst kind of apprehension. Some overprotective parents called their children back as the media started covering the story of the deaths of two young guys almost of the same age.

No one was in the mood to build up spicy love stories after the death of Prakash Bhai, as the fear of an invisible entity killing youngsters for a reason best known to him had driven some of the students into a state of paranoia while the brave ones preferred to treat the impending final examination as their topmost priority, hiding their fear, that lurked at least in one corner of their brave hearts. The usual spurt of activities in a college hostel lapsed into a state of stoic silence, and the jittery boarders counted the number of days left for the examination to end so that, they could go back home safe or at least alive.

With my imagination running wild, I sometimes conjured up the vision of a lady in a white saree and untangled hairs roaming at night, humming the song of death. I was sad because I was really attached to Prakash Bhai. But at the same time, I was secretly fancying the idea of unravelling the truth behind these ghastly deaths like an accomplished detective I had seen in movies or read in crime fiction. Though, it was another matter that, I was no less chicken-hearted than most of my friends. Due to my obsessive preoccupation with these two deaths, I forgot Arun for a while.

A DELICATE BALANCE

Prakash Bhai died yesterday. Some call it suicide and to some of our friends, he just lost his balance in a state of intoxication. I went downstairs where his body was kept before it was sent to the hospital. The I.I.C., with his team, was interrogating his classmates. His body was wrapped in a white cotton cloth stained with blood. He had bled profusely before his death. Prakash Bhai was a wonderful human being. On several occasions, he had offered me a lift while I was coming from my hostel to attend classes in the Arts block, which was at least half a kilometre from my hostel. He was a state-level hockey player. We used to treat him with love, respect and admiration.

His classmates were telling stories about his break-off. But a stable person like Prakash Bhai could never commit suicide for a girl. I have seen him jogging in the sprawling college playground with a tracksuit and a fresh white tee, flaunting toned muscles and sun-tanned skin. From a distance, he looked like a Greek god 'taking the world in his strides'. Prakash Bhai could never kill himself. The entire hostel lapsed into a state of panic and shock after this tragedy. A friend of Prakash Bhai said that he had seen a shadow on the hostel rooftop for two consecutive nights before the death of Prakash Bhai. But I don't believe in these spooky stories cooked up by someone's fertile mind. Rajiv had told me about one such creepy experience he had during his childhood. I had never believed the story of his encounter with somebody, who he thought, could be a spirit, though I have never heard him lying to me. It could be a spectral illusion, which young kids frequently have.

Prakash Bhai's friends believed that the girl had ditched him after she had found a rich guy. They called her a bloody gold digger. But somehow, I could not blame the girl. A day after Prakash Bhai's death, we had a condolence meeting at our hostel. One of the hostel attendants, who was very close to him, cried like a child and then fell on the mattress and lost consciousness. Prakash Bhai was always a man with a genial personality. I was on the verge of tears when the superintendent called me to speak a few lines in his memory. I sat on the mattress, desperately struggling to hold my emotions. Rajiv was also crying.

For days together, I couldn't stop thinking about Prakash Bhai, the manner in which he died, and all the stories being circulated on the campus about his death.

A cool person like him could never fall so desperately in love to the extent of killing himself. Prakash Bhai was anything but a coward or an escapist who couldn't bear the pangs of unrequited love. If he had killed himself, it must have been the realisation of the futility of human relationships, the transience of the emotions one clings to. Death to Prakash Bhai was just another option like life, and he took 'the road less travelled by'.

My mental preoccupation with Prakash Bhai has cost me my studies. I have to forget him for a while and focus on my career. I can't take the "road less travelled by" and lament over my mistake for the rest of my life.

A week has passed since Prakash Bhai's death. Those who were not so close to him preferred to forget the incident just as an accident, ghastly though and resumed their final preparation for the most decisive event of their lives. The rest, who shared some kind of emotional affinity with him, silently mourned his death. It was never easy to forget those warm and tender memories associated with a person who was so affable and protective of the juniors whom he loved.

Deaths like this sometimes expose the fragility of our faith in life and human emotions. But death has a different connotation for me. Basically, death, as I perceive it, is just another state in an endless sequence of events that stretches up to eternity. Death, to me, is not the transcendence of life nor even the negation of its immanence. It's like a journey from one state to another, or it's like pulling down the blinds and making someone invisible as long as we are alive. That was why my mother was staring at the vacant sky with the hope of discovering my father in the clouds or the stars. That was why my brother was silently cursing my father for disappearing from our lives so abruptly, putting the burden of feeding a family of five when he was barely ready to take care of himself. Even as a child, I understood that my mother or my brother were trying to reach out to my father, whom they couldn't see but whose presence they could feel one way or another. I could have been, or I may still be wrong to believe that, the cycle of life doesn't end with death. Sometimes, I was tempted to believe that Prakash Bhai could be watching us all from somewhere, and watching us missing him with so much solemnity and sincerity.

For one week or so, I was not able to concentrate on my studies. I lost interest in everything around me. I saw less, watched less, ate less. There was a disturbing emotional void within me that kept expanding itself every moment. I kept thinking about the agony that keeps tormenting people after someone near and dear disappears from their lives forever. But the only good thing that happened to me was that, I forgot Ruby for a while. I forgot that cold, detached stare she had given me, forgot the feeling of being secondary in someone's life or, to be shockingly honest, being both used and discarded. It was more like curing an ache by hurting another part of your body.

After a long gap, I had the urge to meet my friends and live my life once again, maybe in a boisterous manner, something I had never done before. I felt so bad for giving a cold shoulder to Rajiv. He is still the only person with whom I can easily connect, even though we have so many glaring differences in our characters. For a while, I wanted to be like Rajiv. I wanted to go out with him, breathe some free air, look at this world with defiance, live a life that suits me, and pamper my ego at least for one night.

That night, I took Rajiv to a Dhaba, and for the first time in my life, we drank a bottle of beer each with fried chicken. Rajiv was reluctant. He didn't want to live with the remorse and repentance of luring someone, whom he always found morally formidable, to do something upon which this society has put a sanction. He didn't want to live with the guilt of corrupting the faith of someone like me. But that night, I took control and ironically set the trap into which he fell like an unsuspecting animal.

After dinner, both of us walked back to our hostel. I was carrying the fire in my head, and my legs were practically refusing to carry the burden of my body. I staggered back to the hostel, feeling high like a king but tired like a dog. I used all the swear words I knew, abusing Ruby for what she had done to me. Rajiv asked, "Are you in love with her?" I said, "Just fuck off! She is a bitch. I could have forgiven her, had she played with my feelings. But she played with my self-respect. She made me realise, where I stand in her life. She made me realise my worth. Bloody! Fucking bitch".

Rajiv held my left hand and steadied my teetering feet. He started with a falter but got back his composure and his flair that I always envied and emulated but could never acquire. He said, "I know you won't like my brazenness, but from the very first day I saw you with Ruby, I knew you were in for a big jolt. If you remember, I told you one evening that she simply didn't belong to our world. Getting fascinated with her seductive charm is absolutely normal. But looking for a friend within her is sheer stupidity, and falling in love with her is nothing but insanity. You say that, you are not in love with her. I trust you. But you are still dangerously poised at a point, where you won't be able to deaccelerate your infatuation from turning into love. I am happy that you have not yet fallen in love with her.

But I have still not figured out the nature of the chemistry both of you were sharing while sitting and chatting together. What kind of chemical bond was that, a Co-valent bond or Co-Co-valent bond? Whatever you may call it, to me, it was just a case of pathetic fallacy, and you, to me, are a fragile protagonist of a play, that is tilted heavily towards an unhappy ending. You have to come out of this mess man. This is not what I speak with the conviction of a drunken friend but as a friend, who is moderately drunk yet sane enough to save your ass from getting burnt. As children, we erased so many mistakes we made, even when our hands were not steady. I call it a mistake made by you, and I hope you will erase it forever from your slate".

We were passing through the field in front of our hostel, splashing the patches of accumulated water from an afternoon April shower with our wanton steps. I was ethically wrong but mentally strong. I was happy, and I deserved this happiness in life.

THE RELATIONSHIP RIDDLE

I held myself responsible for not discouraging Arun from doing something he had never approved of. I had seen that strong disapproval in his eyes whenever I came back to the hostel after boozing with my friends.

How could he do such a thing, which he vehemently opposed whenever he had found a close friend in an inebriated state with, what he called,'a repulsive stink' coming from his mouth? All those years, he had been pretty scathing at our friends who wasted their pocket money on buying drinks. How could he forget the position he had so steadfastly taken all along against a habit he considered an act of sinning, a betrayal of the trust of one's parents? For him, drinking poses a threat to the immediate surroundings because a drunken man loses control over himself the moment he gets drunk and passes the rein of his carriage to the dark, subconscious state of his mind, loaded with dark, sinister desires that can not be fulfilled as long as he remembers his social responsibilities. Arun knew he was wrong, yet he was so adamant. Arun knew how vulnerable I was when it came to drinking, and he used me. I would never forgive myself for being so weak and susceptible.

I fell into drinking because I failed in a venture, that brought me nothing but pain, for which no one was responsible except me. I started drinking to be oblivious of the mistake I had made. I started drinking to overcome my sense of guilt, to forget my misery and the painful realisation that, I had behaved stupidly all along. But my case was different because there was no ego, no pride and no sense of loss of identity involved in the whole fiasco. It was just a comedy of errors, and in every comedy, we always find a stupid, gullible character doing something ludicrous and suffering within himself while the world around him laughs at him. I was that stupid, gullible character, and I suffered. Of course, no one knew about my failed love story, save a very few close friends, and when I started drinking, my friends considered it as just one more mistake to spoil a career that never looked promising at any point in time. But Arun was a different human being, sensible and sorted. I knew he had been fighting a war within himself since the day things started going wrong between him and Ruby. It was an invisible war that had left him wounded. He was fighting a battle to uphold his own dignity.

I was never betrayed by anybody except by my illusion, which was inevitable. But his world, which existed in fragments from the beginning, came tumbling down, each part colliding with the other till they were sucked by a black hole, that left a killer void within him. The human within him fell in love with Ruby, and that was not acceptable to the proud intellectual, he believed, he was. His soul was torn apart in a conflict between him and himself, and he started losing a part of himself each time he found himself deeply embroiled in the conflict. A part of himself rejected Ruby, whereas the other part clung to her as if, she was the only one who could give his life a purpose. Arun, Ruby, and Rajiv: We were the three hands of a queer structure that looked like a triangle that didn't have any corner or meeting point. We couldn't meet, yet we were strangely aligned with one another in a strange love story where Arun loved Ruby, and I was, unfortunately, a helpless, dissenting witness. Each time I tried to draw a shape, putting three of us together, I found something grossly abnormal, something missing. It was more like building a structure out of sand on a seashore and waiting patiently till it got washed by a wanton wave so that one could build another.

THE LETTER

Rajiv remains disturbed most of the time. I have seen him sitting on his study table with books spread upon it, yet thinking of something else. Brooding, ruminating or dreaming are never healthy signs, especially at a time when you are taking your final examination. Is Rajiv still single? I have serious doubts about Rajiv's claim of being a carefree single youth. However, this time, Rajiv has got nothing to do with any girl. I have been observing his behaviour since the day after both of us had gone to the Dhaba on the college square and returned home drunk. He has been sulking since that day, kind of avoiding me, very stealthily though. He holds himself responsible for what happened that day. But how can a bright boy like Rajiv be so stupid? I just wanted to have a taste of the forbidden life that I had so religiously shunned and yet got nothing as a reward except a question mark on my identity. I have seen Rajiv and his friends returning to the hostel now and then in a happy state without any moral qualms. I sometimes feel jealous of their happiness, the way they look at everything with total defiance, and the manner in which they celebrate and exult over their successes and failures. The feeling of not being able to be like them, the sense of deprivation I experienced in my attempt to adhere to the self-inflicted discipline, ignited a fire within me, the fire that might destroy all my dreams and ambitions.

I see myself inching closer towards Rajiv, slowly becoming a rebel like him. I have not been indoctrinated by him or anybody. All these years of serious introspection about my career have shown me a world I would love to be a part of, not the world as it exists. I have a fleeting glimpse of that world whenever I try to see it through Rajiv's eyes. The world that I dread, deplore and keep myself away from, is much more fascinating than the world I have created for myself, based on my perception of right and wrong, good, bad or ugly. That evening, accidentally, I became a part of Rajiv's world, and I still hold a part of it, the unused part that I would never return to Rajiv. I am thankful to him, and he should be happy for bringing me out from a dark room where I was playing a game of squash, hitting the balls of doubt, disbelief, self-denial and self-reproach with savage powers till they bounced back with double the velocity to unsettle me. Rajiv helped me live my life only for a day, and I am grateful to him. It was just a part of my experiment with my life, and it's not going to end so soon.

On 24th April, we had a political theory paper. The questions were tough by any standard. Only two of us were seen answering with calm composure. One was me, and the other was the new boy Rohit, who had joined our college late in the wake of his father's transfer. He is brilliant, an avid reader of all kinds of books, and someone who thinks deeply and incisively. I always feel a grudging admiration for him. He is somehow close to Rajiv, but I always stay away from him. You may put the blame on the complex I am suffering from.

After the examination, all of us rushed out of the examination hall to get a bit of respite from the claustrophobic atmosphere, which further deteriorated into a temporary inferno, thanks to the difficulty of the questions. The April heat aggravated the woes of the students, who were sweating profusely in the hall, partly out of heat and partly out of anxiety and fear as the pens they were holding struggled to get the right response from the brain due to the scarcity of proper stimulus from their respective stressed up memories. The ghastly silence in the hall was frequently punctuated by shuffling of legs, wringing of hands, and desperate sighs. The examinees were in a hurry to know how they had done. Rohit, the new boy, and I were surrounded by students. I saw Ruby standing on the edge of the corridor, her pretty face clouded by her desperation and dilemma. After discussing the questions with my friends, I nonchalantly walked to Ruby and wished her. She was almost on the verge of tears as she could not get a single question from her list of prepared questions. I patiently listened to summaries of the answers and left the corridor with a few consoling words. To be honest, hers was more than an average performance and considering the standard of the question, it was okay. After a few days, I found a letter for me in the letter box. I was surprised, not shocked. It was from Ruby.

Dear Arun,

Don't be surprised to receive this stupid letter from me. I know you have put up with my delinquent behaviour for almost two years, and you have never complained. I hope you will put up with the last instalment of my stupidity as patiently as you have done before. Today, I don't want to juggle with words or expressions to take you away from the truth, that has been stinging me like a bug for the last few months, and I need to tell you the truth because, a wonderful human being like you, deserves to hear nothing, but the truth.

Right from my childhood, I was brought up in a liberated society. My father would always remain busy with his business and my mother with kitty parties and socialising, leaving three young children under the custody of a maid. She was just a caretaker, whose prime duty was our physical well-being, but we were all emotionally famished. Gradually, we learnt to fend for ourselves. Being loved, cajoled or pampered were feelings alien to us. Whenever I saw our maid treating her children with love and care, I used to feel jealous of those lucky kids.

When I was enrolled in a public school, I was so happy! I was never a bright student, a truth that you know so well. But as a cute and pretty kid, I always got attention from my teachers and my friends. As I grew up, I got used to a life crowded with people who were neither my family members nor my relatives. But the attention I received from them did matter to me. I grew up as a liberated child, who knew so well what she needed from this life. So, I spent most of my time partying with my friends. I had fun, but I could not get emotionally attached to anyone. It's not about being or not being in love. It's about my mental deficiency in channelling my emotions. I lacked the emotional quotient, so essential for establishing a permanent bond with someone. I started living a highly compartmentalised life, where only I could be the boss. I was the mover and shaker.

I had reached a dead end when we met. During the first few days, it was your intellectual exuberance that kept me fascinated. I was really scared to talk to you in those early days, because of the fear of getting caught. I didn't want you to know how shallow I am. I was, and I still am, in a state of awe whenever I discuss things with you. My curiosity to know what stuff you are made of pulled me towards you. But unfortunately, it was more like the inquisitiveness of a small child about an exotic toy. I wanted to own you, keep you in my closet and show my proud possession to those like me. But I got the biggest jolt of my life when you reacted against my wanton ways of dealing with you.

My biggest mistake was my inability to see the human being within you, so different from me, someone who has a mind of his own, someone who knows what he is, someone who can lead but never be led. My biggest mistake again was that, I thought I could treat you the way I treat my friends, just as a fascinated entity who can rally around me as and when needed. I was always wrong. I completely misread you, misunderstood you, and finally broke you like a doll with my stupid hands. I shouldn't have done that. It was all my mistake. But I can't mend my ways. You deserve much better friends and much better people in your life. Forgive me, if you can. I won't blame you, if you don't. The time I have spent with you will remain the most beautiful hours of my life. I can't call you my friend. But you are the most wonderful thing that has happened to me. Stay happy and blessed.

***Ruby*.**

I read the letter once, then reread it. The letter was honest and dispassionate. It told me everything I knew, but dreaded to hear. I sat on my bed, my head resting on the pillow and thought for a long, long time. I was wrong from the beginning, wrong in reading human nature. I don't blame Ruby for that. Rather, I appreciate her honesty and the fact that, she has been straightforward about her feelings for me. I should have dissociated myself from her world long ago. But somehow, I was delusional, and now I have to pay a price for that. I asked myself a question which, I had never had the courage to ask myself. 'Was I ever in love with her'? She has certainly intruded into my mind, disturbing the rock-solid conviction I had about myself as an unshakable entity with the self-belief, which stood like a wall, transparent like glass, but impregnable like iron. Why did I allow the iron doors to swing open to give entry to someone, who was not meant for me? I have to share this letter with Rajiv. He is the only guy who can save me from crumbling down with self-pity. On many occasions, he has been brazenly sensible while giving a remark that I have resented in the past. But beneath that nonchalant exterior, I have noticed a sensitive human being, someone who can barter his head and heart to save a friend in distress.

THE PAPER BOAT

I was not surprised that day with Arun's reaction. Any other person could have taken Ruby's letter as an acknowledgement of his superiority, which Ruby had meticulously projected. She hadn't jumbled up her feelings, caught in a wave of guilt or repentance. The letter had been drafted, not written, with the remarkable astuteness that only a girl like Ruby could do. It concealed much more than it revealed, and Ruby had done that with perfection. But Arun had a brilliant mind. He knew what the letter was all about. It was a splendid disclaimer about one's detachment in a relationship that was based upon misunderstanding and misconception between two persons with diametrically opposing orientations. Unfortunately, it came from the wrong person to the wrong person at the wrong time.

Arun was trying to put on a strong front. But I knew how brittle he was. He had seen a lot in life. I wondered, how he could survive those string of tragedies. I certainly didn't want him to suffer more. I was sure that he was confused about his relationship with Ruby. He was more like a small child, who had made a paper boat with all his love and care and set it afloat with the hope that it would reach where it should, but ended up getting a crumpled piece of paper on the same river bank, from where he had put it on water.

I didn't want to speak outright against Ruby. I didn't want to tell him how bleak the scenario looked. I just wanted him to survive, what I thought, could be the final incursion on his heart. We had only a few more days to stay here on this campus. After that, we would all drift apart and sail to our respective new destinations. Time and distance can heal the nastiest of the wounds. I wanted Arun to overcome the trauma like a gallant found in early eighteenth-century romances. I wanted him to treat the letter as lightly as he could. During my childhood, I often used to score low in mathematics and cry a lot after being reprimanded by my father, but I forgot it completely the very next day. Arun just got one sum wrong: it's all about one's perception. The wheel of life doesn't come to a grinding halt with one setback. Life has to move on. Nobody is indispensable in life. I suddenly remembered Saswati. I needed to talk to her. Together, I thought, we could discover a cure for the ailing prince.

I hadn't talked to her for months. Both of us were busy with the last part of our final examination. I couldn't discuss the issue with her at her home. I had to invite her to Vijaya café where we could talk over a mug of coffee. The prospect of meeting Saswati, that too for a valid cause, made me happy for a moment. I took Arun to the theatre to watch 'The Sound of Music'. While coming back, Arun did not look that unhappy.

A SOLUTION, FINALLY

I met Saswati nearly after two months. In a hostel, the students normally did not have access to telephones, moreover, the parents of the girls during those days were pretty conservative. So, a phone call from a boy posing as a friend to their daughter was never enthusiastically accepted. Of course, Saswati's father was not so prudish. He never resented our entry into their house.

Saswati gave me a warm smile as we met near a book depot beside the restaurant. She was wearing a wine-coloured kameez and a white salwar, and she looked elegant in that outfit. Saswati was not beautiful in the conventional sense of the term, but the reflection of goodness on her face accentuated her beauty. I was tempted to feel sad for a while, thinking why I had not fallen in love with her, though falling in love meant to me a fall into a pit, where one could never find a rope long and strong enough to pull me out. I cursed myself for having such a thought in my mind.

The restaurant was not very crowded. It was one of the two restaurants in College Square, serving authentic South Indian food. Saswati ordered one masala Dosha and a cup of filter coffee. They were her favourites, and I ordered a plate of Boda with coffee. We ate in silence. She was relishing the crisp Dosha, and I was happy with the delicious combination of Boda, Sambar and Chutney on the platter. With a sip of coffee, I told her about Ruby's letter and Arun's reaction. She didn't seem surprised. She said, "I knew. We all knew it was going to happen one day. I am happy that Arun, at least, got to know the truth, and I hope, it's not too late. A guy like Arun can't be deeply involved with a bitch like Ruby". She was apologetic about using the word 'bitch' so liberally in a public place. But I was happy to hear it from her. I was worried for my friend, and I wanted a way out to help him survive this emotional ordeal. I was optimistic that Saswati could come up with something new, may be an innovative suggestion to help Arun attain a sort of self-reconciliation, help him heal his wounded ego or restore his dwindling self-belief. Saswati belonged to a rare breed, calm, contemplative and blessed with the uncanny knack of not losing one's cool even in a highly provocative situation. I was confident that, Arun would certainly consider any suggestion from Saswati because he used to like her too.

As the cup of coffee was getting empty with every sip, Saswati was sitting there, deeply immersed in her thoughts, perhaps trying to figure out a working solution that would make life easier for Arun. I was staring at her with hopeful eyes and an increasing palpitation in my heart. "Why don't you take him out somewhere for a day or two and just have the typical boyish fun there, with no one to keep a watch on you? Of course, with the final paper just a few days away, he won't be keen to go out anywhere. Anyways, you can suggest a plan for an outing during the summer with him and two of your best buddies. He might find the idea exciting, and that would keep his mind preoccupied for a few days, and the thoughts of Ruby would take a back seat. All you can do right now is, keep him engaged. He is passing through the toughest phase of his life and you have to rescue the drowning Icarus. Stay with him, take him out for walks, movies and musical nights, and keep him engaged. Talk to him about his life at the JNU campus and tell him how much you are going to miss him. That works, Rajiv." I felt relieved for a while; at least, I got something to work on. Nothing works better than distracting a suffering mind with some funny allurement, however frivolous it may seem to be. I thanked Saswati for being there with me, whenever I needed her the most. She smiled wryly and said, "I am happy that you are so worried about Arun. But he is not the only sufferer in this world. There are others, too, who need and deserve that much concern. You don't have any idea, how gratifying this would be for them," she spoke with a chuckle.

As we left the restaurant, she paid the bill, knowing fully well that, this was the last week of the month, when spendthrifts like me had to move around with empty wallets. She got into an auto rickshaw, and from inside the rickshaw, she waved at me. I once again cursed myself for not being in love with Saswati. I wrote a poem that night.

SO MANY THINGS TO DO AND SO LITTLE TIME

Lying on my bed with books and notes spread around me, I read Ruby's letter. This is perhaps my hundredth attempt to understand a brief letter comprising ten to twelve sentences. However, with each reading, I prefer to postpone the self-drawn conclusion. The deconstructive angle gets entangled in a web of words, the multiplicity of meanings they generate and the deep dark void they create within, tickling my hope and hopelessness. I hate myself for still not being tired of reading and rereading her letter.

Just one more week to go before we take our final paper and leave the college, the hostel, our friends and the myriad memories associated with this campus that never sleeps.

One more week in my hand to come out of this shit and get ready for a brighter future. I am sure, I will get one more scholarship to fulfil my dreams and those of Dhani Sir, and bring a smile to the pale, shrivelled face of my mother; ask her not to keep looking at the sky at night because the sky offers us nothing. I would love to tell my brother that, the painful days are going to be over soon. I folded the letter and kept it under my pillow. I have to meet Rajiv and discuss the prospect of joining any other elite coaching institution at an affordable cost. I should talk to Rohit and seek his guidance. I have so many things to do and so little time to do them all.....

It's an April afternoon. I peeped through the windows of my room. In the sky, I saw dark, moisture-laden clouds gathering with ominous intensity to overpower the setting sun. There will be rain very soon, accompanied by thunder, lightning, wind and hailstones. I remember how, during my childhood, all the siblings used to rush to our courtyard to gather hailstones whenever it rained in April. We had never seen Ice Cream Wallas in our village, selling ice candies to kids, nor did we have the money to buy them. While chewing the little white hailstones and feeling the biting chill as they melted down in our oral cavities, there was always a strange feeling of happiness mixed with excitement. While looking through the window at the dark sky, I missed my village.

When Rajiv came from behind, I was lost in my thoughts. I was startled when I felt his hand on my shoulder. I was startled to see him standing there with a queer expression on his face. "What's up, man?" he asked me. "All good?" I nodded my head. Rajiv looked happy and excited. "Let's go downstairs to the canteen to have a cup of tea." It was not a bad proposal, considering the weather outside. A hot cup of tea, when it's pouring outside is something I always relish. Rajiv took me to the canteen and ordered two cups of tea. Then he told me, "My father had come today. He was really keen to meet you. But I didn't want to disturb you because I know how serious you have been all these days for the final examination. By the way, he has asked me to invite you to spend the first week of the vacation at our place. There is one incentive for you from my side if you honour this invitation from my father. Remember, he doesn't invite many people to our home. We may spend the second week at your place". The proposal was enticing, but what left me perplexed was the fact that uncle (Rajiv's father) came and went away without meeting me. That had never happened earlier. He always believed that I was the only person who could bring about a transformation in Rajiv's life. Whenever he comes to meet

Rajiv, he never goes back without meeting me. As a village school teacher, he has never appreciated Rajiv's attitude towards life. I had no other reason to disbelieve Rajiv. I got mentally ready to spend a week at Rajiv's place in the fourth week of May.

THE FUTURE UNCERTAIN........

I was so eager to share my happiness with Saswati. But meeting her when the final paper was barely a week away, was impossible. The last two months had been nothing short of an expiation for me. I had to study at least twelve hours a day to put in a semblance of a fight in the toughest battle I had ever faced in my life. It was almost a policy decision taken by all my truant friends to keep ourselves alienated for at least two months and extricate ourselves from the smothering frustration of not being able to deliver when it mattered most. We were getting ready to keep ourselves happy with a face-saving B+ grade so that we would be able to face our parents with some self-respect. We all worked hard to salvage our sinking pride, heal our battered ego and leave the campus not with a head stooping low or a shoulder drooping down. I was not worried about Arun's studies. We all knew Arun and Rohit would have a neck-to-neck fight, with Rohit having a slight edge over Arun.

I knew Saswati would get married after doing her post-graduation. She was not so ambitious when it came to career building. It was not that she did not have her dreams. But she was perfectly grounded. Her parents, too, didn't have high expectations from her. Saswati was not exactly bright, but she was smart and intelligent with a great sense of humour. On many occasions, I had watched her transforming a dull classroom into a lively and hilarious one with her characteristic witty observations. Most of our teachers liked her too. But the sense of humour or underutilised intelligence doesn't help anyone get a good grade or a job.

I was getting ready for a long, boring post-exam sabbatical. I knew it would be tough for me to stay away from my friends when there was no guarantee that we would all be reunited once again. But that's how life goes on, like the waves on the sea, sometimes hitting the shore with brutal madness, sometimes retreating like a fugitive. No one knows what tomorrow holds for them. I was not mentally ready to take a job so soon. But I had to get a seat in any good university to do my post-grad. My future looked so ruffled to me, like my hair. I looked at the twilight sky to find a shooting star to make a wish. Man's destiny and destination are not always the same.

I closed my eyes and kept musing, "At home, I will sit with my mother while she cooks rice in an earthen pot mounted upon the earthen oven, and I will talk to her about Arun, Akash, Vikash, Rohit, Abinash, Raju, Rasik and others. I won't be able to talk to her about Saswati. The idea of a boy and a girl being friends with each other was still not acceptable in our society, especially when you came from a rural background. I will spread a mattress under the mango tree in our courtyard and sleep under its shade on a hot summer afternoon. I will catch fish from our pond with a net and show my mother a live fish wriggling in my grip to free itself. I will assist our domestic help while feeding the cattle. While staring at the star-studded sky, I will miss the campus life I have spent with my friends whom I had once met as strangers". I sensed someone standing behind me.

THE ENCOUNTER

I was sitting in the study centre of Kanika Library today. This is perhaps the only library that boasts of an impressive collection of books and journals with a huge reading room to accommodate more than three hundred students at a time.

The library remains open till nine P.M. in the evening, so that, the hostel boarders can collect their study materials even during the evening. We frequently come to this place in the evening as we keep ourselves busy, attending lectures during the day. Since we had just one more paper to go and students from poor or lower-middle-class families could not afford to buy essential reference books, I sometimes had to come during the daytime as our classes had been suspended long since due to the ongoing Final Examinations.

I was sitting in the second row after collecting a copy of Leviathan: Political Philosophy by Thomas Hobbe from the counter. As I was flipping through the pages, I heard a familiar voice from my back. When I looked back, I saw Rubby, but she was not alone. She was sitting with Biswajit, a tall and handsome boy from the psychology department. Ruby was surprised to find me sitting just one row ahead of her. My presence was a big dampener for her. She didn't even wish me and pretended as if, she was deeply engrossed in reading a book, though I had heard her talking to Biswajit just a while ago. Never in my life had I been so cleverly ignored.

Biswajit is a decent boy who is immensely liked by everyone. His father works as a senior bureaucrat in the office of the Hon'ble Chief Minister. Biswajit comes to college every day riding his Yamaha Rx100 bike. But unlike all other students from rich families, Biswajit does not exude any high-handedness or arrogance in his behaviour. He is always friendly and warm with all his batchmates, no matter how rich or poor they may be. Developing a crush on Biswajit is absolutely normal, and I don't blame Ruby for that. I know, Biswajit is no Casanova, and he doesn't flirt with girls. He is the coolest guy I have ever seen on this campus. But what I found disconcerting was the way Ruby behaved when she saw me. Biswajit waved at me, and I waved back. To be honest, I felt jealous for a while and angry too, not with Biswajit, because I always admired this guy for being nice to us all. I remember he had once arranged a VIP pass for all of us to watch an India Vs England one-day match. After the match, he invited us to his home and gave us a Biriyani Party on their lawn. It was an all-boys affair. For a while, I felt like pitying Biswajit. But actually, I was pitying myself.

I could not focus on my studies. I felt deeply disturbed, as if someone had razed all the admiration, that all my classmates had for me. I felt like rushing out of the study centre, confronting Ruby and asking her why she had played with my feelings. But my mind went blank for a while. I stood hooked, holding the book in my hand. Biswajit gave me a curious glance. How could he know what was happening inside me? I deposited the book on the counter and left the study centre in a hurry. What exactly was my problem? Ruby was never in love with me. She made it very clear in her letter that, I was just one of her classmates, and our relationship was based on her respect and admiration for me, which are not always the essential preconditions for falling in love. Respect, love, and admiration most often walk side by side, with one consolidating the other to build a perfect relationship based on trust and understanding. My inflated self-esteem was left deflated by someone, who knew her priorities. She is so sorted, so mature, deceptively sweet but steadfastly decisive. Rajiv seemed so right that day.

I ran back to my hostel and almost flung myself on my bed. I wanted to cry, but there were no tears in my eyes. I felt like meeting Rajiv. Perhaps he can tell me why I feel so ripped apart. Am I making a mountain out of a molehill and aggravating my problems when they do not exist? But why do I feel so much agony within me? Why so much turmoil? I want to share everything with Rajiv. But I am afraid of his hard-hitting wisdom and his obvious solution, which I cannot accept because I am not like him. I am not an escapist. I have tried once to dissolve my frustrations in a mug of beer. That only worked for a night. I woke up the next morning with a heavy head, feeling groggy, and the hangover stayed till afternoon, spoiling my day. I felt like going back to my home and spending a couple of days with my mother. Perhaps I will get back the tears only when I place my head on her lap, smell her sweat-mixed body odour, and feel her coarse, bony hand caressing my body. How much I wish to tell her about the mistake I have made! Only she can get me back from this no man's land. Only she can detoxify me with her benign touch. That's what love can do to somebody. But how can I go home right now, when the final paper is barely a few days away?

THE TURBULENT WAVES

I turned back to see Arun's roommate standing behind me. There was a tell-tale sign of exasperation in his eyes. He was a bit concerned and agitated because Arun had turned out to be a liability for him, especially during the crucial final examination period. He told me Arun had been behaving strangely of late, barely coming out of his room and not talking to anybody. I was shocked to hear that, he had, in the meantime, gone to Puri with three of our classmates, whom he had always disliked for their lack of moral scruples, and stayed there till late evening, sitting on the beach, refusing to leave even when it was time to catch the evening train. Those three guys, who had never helped anyone in their lives, had to break their cannons about interpersonal relationships and practically dragged him out of the beach when he was stubborn about spending a night there. "I want to speak to the waves about my woes. I know the waves never disappoint anyone. You guys go away. I want to stay here tonight."

One of the agitated young men in a state of inebriation cursed him with the filthiest slang. But Arun was unmoved; there was something complex and mystifying about his body language. Perhaps he was lost in his own world and refused to hear sounds from the world around him. Perhaps he was in a state of deep hallucination, and that was scary. The three boys were convinced that such strange behaviour could be the earliest manifestation of insanity or may be undiagnosed schizophrenia, though they were in a hurry to agree on one opinion for the sake of their safety. Bringing Arun back to the hostel was a daunting task and they accomplished it with admirable tenacity, but total lack of sensitivity. I didn't know, how I would have behaved had I been in their situation. But one thing became so evident: Arun had to be handled with utmost care. I met three of my friends who were also close to Arun and we went in a group to meet him.

We knocked on the door several times and finally called him loudly. After five minutes, he opened the door. I was completely aghast to see the person standing before me. He looked like a ghost of his former self, with dishevelled hair, an unkempt beard, and a torn and dirty vest. He was not happy to see us. He asked me roughly, "What happened? Why are you here with these three? Why did you disturb my sleep? What do you think? Is the exam over"? There was a volley of questions he fired at us with an aggression I had never seen during those four years. All of us looked at each other and said sorry to him with a degree of politeness that a friend never uses while talking to another friend because we didn't want to escalate the situation. I could read the insanity in his eyes, the potentially dangerous withdrawal syndrome, the constipated feeling of desperation. He behaved so differently as if he did not know any of us. Was he slowly slipping into a state of degenerative amnesia? I couldn't leave him unattended in that state. I didn't know what exactly had gone wrong. Was it Ruby again?

THE BURIAL OF THE SOUL

I sat on the beach, a few yards away from Pramod, Dillip and Tarun. They were sipping three bottles of

Haywards 5000 in a secluded corner of the beach. They had offered me one bottle too, but I was not in the right frame of mind. The only person with whom I had taken alcohol only once was Rajiv. But Rajiv is so different from these guys. When Rajiv gets drunk, he speaks like an intellectual; his articulation is so lucid, not like any of the meaningless blabbering of these three drunken guys. I sometimes feel amused to hear a strain of thoughts that sound like the lines from a melancholic poem. I admire the ways he amalgamates disparate ideas to build up coherence, even when he is drunk. I know Rajiv lives and dies every moment because of his failed relationship with his father. I know both of them love each other in a certain inexplicable manner that I fail to comprehend sometimes and, therefore, give the benefit of the doubt to Rajiv. I wish I could have been like Rajiv. But I am not like him. I am like myself, someone who loves to hide a part of his dark world within himself, yet hates himself for being so consciously discreet. That habit of mine has brought me today to the brink of a catastrophe.

I looked at the waves of the sea in the growing darkness. They all looked sad and lonely. Were they crying, banging their heads on the cold, indifferent sandy shore of the sea? I felt like getting deep into the sea and getting lost there, till I rediscovered myself in another world, where I could live happily with the people I love, where the dark shadow of someone like Ruby would not upset me. I saw the waves coming towards me. I was thrilled to see this reciprocal gesture. I wanted to ride on the waves. When I was getting ready for the final plunge, three pairs of strong male hands pulled me away and brought me back to the shore using savage force. I had never liked them earlier, but I had never hated them with so much intensity when they were happy with the thought that they were my rescuers. In fact, they killed me then and there and buried my soul deep within the cold, grey sands of the beach.

My story ended that day with a tragic tryst with my destiny. While throwing a handful of sand at the receding waves of the sea, I threw all my dreams, ambitions, and love for my family and friends. The madness of the waves turned me into an obdurate entity, divested of everything that I had always found so precious in life. When I came back, I was just a beingless being with an empty mind and a dead soul.

THE BLACKHOLE

I distinctly remember the day, though thirty long years of life that preceded it with so many twists and turns, happiness and sorrow, disease and recovery, had slowly ushered in a lingering sense of oblivion. As I see myself today, a long battle for thirty long years has left me tired and worn out, and death is perhaps the only inevitable option to cleanse the heavily scribbled slate of memory distorted by time. But that day has been haunting me for the last thirty years, the unerasable trail of tragedy written on the slate. It looked so bright and vicious, like the painted monster mask worn by a child for whom happiness lies in making other helpless children of his age jittery. The day still brings nightmares to me, a middle-aged man counting the blessings of his life amid the clashes and conflicts, acceptance and reconciliation, that make life a bagful of oxymorons, so unpalatably palatable and so palatably unpalatable.

Coming back to the day, it was the final day of the final examination, a hot and humid summer afternoon. Most of us left the hostel after a tense lunch. The mess secretary had asked the manager to serve fish and curd to all the examinees. The general secretary of the hostel was caring enough to stick a beautiful poster above the entrance gate, wishing us all good luck. They were such nice and caring gestures, immensely gratifying but not adequately reciprocated, because the fear of not being able to deliver when it mattered most, was killing most of us from the inside. I went to Arun's room. I wanted to accompany him to the examination hall because, I knew, he was not in a stable state. I knocked on the door, and after a few minutes, he came out, decently dressed. He looked cool and composed. I felt so relieved to see him behaving in a normal way. I asked him to sit on my bicycle carrier, and I paddled all the way to the three-storeyed commerce block, where we were to be accommodated as per the seating chart to take the final paper of the final examination. To me, it was a painful preparedness to invade the last strategic configuration of the supposedly last battle of our life against destiny at a time, when the fear of a retreat looked so frighteningly imminent.

I looked at Arun's face. It was a blank face displaying no emotion. How could he be so normal today? Could it be the signs of the proverbial lull before a storm brewing up on the not-so-distant horizon to lash our tiny, compact world made up of a four-year-long bond of love and friendship? I was struggling to read the expression on his face. I had a disturbing premonition that, something was wrong somewhere, and I could not read it properly. Moreover, I had my own preoccupation, the natural nervousness before entering the examination hall. I shook hands with him and hugged him before we parted ways to enter the examination hall. He hugged me tight and hugged me hard as if, he didn't want to let me go. Then he hastened his steps, leaving me standing there in a state of bewilderment, with an incomprehensible sense of foreboding. Slowly, I moved to my assigned room, my eyes still searching for him.

The questions were difficult but not unattainable. I tried to write my answer utilising all the resources I had accumulated during the last two months of my desperate endeavour to avoid the possibility of a debacle that seemed so inevitable two months ago. But perhaps I had impressed the almighty, at least with a semblance of sincerity of my intention. I wrote all the answers, sitting patiently for three hours on the wooden bench as my pen glided forward with unprecedented spontaneity and flair until I reached the last page of the answer book[1]. After the final bell was given, I stood up and submitted my answer script, stretched my stiff limbs, and heaved a sigh of huge relief. "It's not going to be that bad. I will get through." A whip of warm air of an April evening brushed against my cheeks.

As I walked out of the commerce block, I thought of Arun. It was not that I was worried about his performance in the examination. I just wanted to meet him and talk to him over a cup of tea. My eyes swept over the crowd of students streaming out of the hall, some beaming with a feeling of triumph and others with sad, heavy faces. I could not see him as the rush started thinning down. I met Saswati. She was talking to a few girls. When she saw me, she waved at me. She looked happy that day. I asked her if she had seen Arun. She shook her head. We talked for a while about the plans she had for her future. She said, perhaps jokingly, "I want to get married soon and have a family with a dozen kids and a loving husband". I couldn't believe her, but I didn't take her seriously either. For a while, I thought about Saswati and felt bad for her for being so outrageously callous to her. She had all along been a wonderful friend, someone who had tried very hard to understand my predicament. In all probability, this could be our last meeting or the penultimate one. I felt a lump in my throat as I spoke, "We may not meet again. But thank you for being such a wonderful friend. Thank you for handling an idiot like me so well. Even if we do not meet, I will always remember you for not deserting me despite my reckless response. Whenever I needed you, you were always there. You know, fame has a way of fading, and friendships disappearing, when they are needed the most. That is something so endearingly special about you". Saswati held my hand and said, "You are a good guy, Rajiv. When goodness is perceived as a stereotype, it ceases to be goodness. You have always been a very special friend to me, a friendship I wish to continue. But I know it's not going to happen. My wishes will always be with you. Do well, Rajiv. You can and you must. Just understand the difference between being and becoming. Have your dream and fulfil it. If it is not for you, then at least for those you love." She was still holding my hand. This was the first time in my life a girl had held my hands with her delicate fingers. I could feel my heart pumping blood faster. It might be for the last time in my life. I threw the most difficult question to the vacant but amorphous universe, "Am I truly in love with her?" The silence that followed it was perhaps the answer to my question.

I said goodbye to Saswati. I felt so sad and low as the prospect of meeting her once again in life didn't look bright. Then I thought for a while, if it is so difficult to say goodbye to a girl with whom, I didn't even get the chance to spend more than a couple of hours a day, then how difficult it would be to say the final goodbye to Arun, Bikash, Akash, Abinash, Raju and Rasik. They were the guys with whom I shared everything that a man could share with another man. I was feeling sad, perplexed and dejected. I pedalled slowly along the dark metal path leading straight to my hostel with a mind laden with weird thoughts and, to top them all, more weird feelings. As I was about to turn towards my hostel, I found Ruby eating Paanipuri with Biswajit on one corner of the crossroads. I saw the wrong girl with the wrong boy at the wrong time and realised, why Arun's face looked so pallid, though he was neatly dressed to appear in the last paper in the final examination. I looked at Ruby with surprise and disdain and cast a sympathetic glance at her latest victim, a boy who had been an epitome of decency and goodness.

I hastened my steps towards my hostel. I wanted to meet Arun. I stopped for a while and looked at the enchanted castle where our sweet damsels in distress stayed. Looking at one half-closed window, I spoke indistinctly, "Wait, we will come tonight to stage the last act of the drama you have been watching for two long years". I remembered a few lines from the beautiful ballad *The Highway Man*:' Wait for me in moonlight, I will come to thee in moonlight, even if hell bars the way'. I wanted to compose a parody of it and sing tonight, drumming an old guitar with snapped strings, and this would be my farewell song. But before that, I had to meet Arun and send him home tomorrow, if I noticed any deterioration in his mental state.

When I reached the entrance of the hostel, I was greeted by a few juniors. One guy told me that they had arranged a special midnight get-together for the outgoing seniors, and they had also obtained the permission of the hostel superintendent, who had given his consent with a condition. The condition was; there would be no alcohol nor viewing of porn in the common room, which some students were prone to do, taking advantage of the stillness of the night and the remote possibility of any surprise check. I was happy for a while. One of my friends, the son of a member of the legislative assembly who was with me, whispered in my ear that he had kept a bottle of single-malt whiskey gifted by a businessman to his father. The proposal could have been very exciting on any other day. But I was really worried for Arun, especially after discovering Ruby with Biswajit. He might have seen them on his way. I wanted to meet Arun and talk to him. Moreover, we had two more days in hand, and I didn't want to share a minute of it with anyone else except Arun, Bikash and Akash. Bikash, Akash and I were fondly branded as the three musketeers of the campus. Of course, Arun was an exception. But he preferred to hang out with us only when he had time to chill out with his friends, and that happened occasionally.

I stood in front of Arun's room and knocked on his door softly. His roommate opened the room. He was getting ready to watch the night show of 'The Never Ending Story', a wonderous fantasy that received global accolades as a superb fantasy epic, playing with a full house at a nearby theatre. He wanted to take Arun along with him, but Arun stubbornly declined to accompany him. His roommate left, worried, irritated and angry. I saw Arun sleeping on his bed. He was certainly not asleep. But he didn't get up to talk to me, ask me how I had done in my paper and what were my plans for the night. I found a strange inertia on his face. It looked placid, like a sheet of white paper. I told him rather authoritatively, "Wake up and get ready. We have a party tonight, the last party we are going to have in this hostel. You have to drink with me tonight, and I won't let you give me a slip."

He gave me a strange smile, a deep sardonic one. He stretched his hands and held mine gently. Then he exhaled deeply and muttered with a muffled voice. "Sorry yaar, I feel so weak and low. My paper didn't go that well. They say, there is light at the end of the tunnel, but I find none. I lost the battle, the biggest battle of my life. I am a loser, and fate never treats a loser kindly. This is the lesson my life has taught me in a hard way". He sobbed as he spoke. I had never seen him breaking down to that degree. I was aware of his distress in his childhood. I always knew him as a warrior, a winner, someone who could face all odds with the grit and toughness of a soldier. I knew him as someone who neither gave up nor gave in so easily. I didn't want to attend the midnight revelry without him. I wanted to stay with him, talk to him, console him and tell him stories about our togetherness. I didn't want to leave him in this dismal state. But as usual, he had his ways. He told me mildly not to disturb him. When I refused to leave, he was almost rude. I left his room, leaving him on his bed, vacantly staring at the ceiling fan, whirring out the hot air around a 10ftx12ft room. I was hurt but not angry.

A TREE SHEDS ITS LAST LEAF

I gave up the idea of meeting my friends in the evening. The idea was so irresistible for a while but went down like the drooping mercury in winter. So did my desire to attend the late-night party and get drunk before going home to live a life I detested just to keep my parents happy. I sat on the parapet and looked at the star-studded sky. The moon looked so lonely, though surrounded by millions of twinkling stars. Fleets of clouds resembling thin white muslin cloths were hurrying back to their home. I found myself seated on one of them. I recalled my childhood and the diseases that gave my father sleepless nights. He was just afraid of letting me live a life like others because, I was always so different: sick, frail and fragile. I felt bad for misunderstanding my father. I thought of Arun and his nightmarish childhood, the sense of deprivation that had become part of his life, those few days he had spent in an orphanage. I tried to recall all those stories he had told me about his mother, elder brother, and sisters, as well as the stories of their afflictions and their survival. In a sense, we were like two boys running along the sides of a railway track, throwing stones and making faces at each other. Then suddenly, one of us tried to cross the track to meet the other but failed to hear the whistle of the speeding train.

At 10 p.m., the inmates from the Junior batches came to me in a group. They practically dragged me out to join the party. I could hear the microphone blaring harshly in the common room. To be honest, I succumbed to the temptation of sharing the last instalment of my ecstasy in a congregation that one could call a miniature version of contemporary rave parties. Everyone was in a state of frenzy, in a state of haste, as if the doomsday was around the corner and there would be no celebration after that. I got drunk and then danced with passion, with intoxication, celebrating the sheer triumph of life. And I forgot my friend, languishing in his lonely room in a terrible state of mental agony, whom one could empathise with only when he had been going through the same turmoil of being at the receiving end of the life that had been so unkind to him. I forgot the person who had held my hand and led me along when I was on the verge of ruining my life. I had almost abandoned my dearest friend at a time when he was fighting a terrible battle within himself when I should have been with him. Because, I was the only person, whom he had always loved, trusted and fallen back on during the most difficult hours in his life. I sinned that night and it could never be forgiven, no matter how painfully prolonged my repentance was going to be.

It was around 12.30 a.m. when I heard someone shrieking from the first floor. I could hear the loud banging sounds as if someone was desperately knocking on a door while calling someone by his name. Someone turned off the sound of the microphone. I could hear Akash calling Arun. It sounded like a distress cry. I ran to the first floor, forgetting for a while how unstable I was. I saw Akash standing in front of his room and kicking the doors with all his force. When he saw me, he broke down. "He is not opening the door. I have been trying for the last twenty minutes. He is not responding. There is something awfully wrong, Rajiv. When did you see him last?" he was getting hysterical. Everything looked so blurry, so fuzzy to me. The spell of alcohol had kept me in its thrall. There was confusion all around: the proverbial chaos in the hell. I stood motionless, enveloped by a disturbing cacophony, unable to understand a single syllable of the animated discussions of my friends who were standing there in tense anticipation. The hostel guard came, holding an iron rod in his hand and broke open the door by pushing the rod through the narrow opening between the alignment of the twin doors of Arun's room with a savage force. Akash shrieked loudly as the door creaked open, leaving us all in a state of shock, deep, nerve-shattering and frightening. There, inside the room, we saw him hanging from the damned ceiling fan, his neck tilted to his right, and the tongue viciously darted out from his mouth. **Arun finally hanged himself!!!!**

A part of me melted down, diluting the effects of wine on me. My drooping eyelids fluttered open with shock and disbelief. Most of the boarders closed their eyes in an unknown terror, but I could not. It was a catastrophe for me that shook the ground below my feet. I looked at his face, trying to gauge the pain he might have gone through a minute before his death, when the spine would have given in, choking the windpipe to cause a painful death. Horrible he looked with all the pain and suffering written on a face that normally looked so bright with his characteristic goodness and intelligence. But what was more painful was the sign of giving up the battle and retreating from the field, when he had almost made it. I saw a sheet of paper lying on the ground.

Since it had become a crime scene, we were waiting for the police to come and dismantle the body and send it for postmortem. We were struggling to accept the fact that Arun killed himself. It was hard to believe and even harder to accept. Why did he kill himself when God was merciful enough to alleviate the pains of his past and offer him a life full of promises? Why did he sell his soul to the devil so easily? Was it for the girl or his wounded ego? Was it for the sense of failure or the feeling of being utilised and then ignored? Arun killed himself to settle a score with his very own self. There was anger building up among our friends. But I told them to cool down because Arun had been behaving strangely off late. He was delusional, which eclipsed his rationality. We had witnessed three gory deaths within a short span of one and half months, and they were all so shockingly disturbing, so bizarre, shrouded in a mystery that none could unravel, and they would remain a mystery to all of us as long as we live.

I dived through the layers and layers of darkness, trying to figure out what went wrong. I could have and should have saved his life had I acted with a little patience. I cursed my lack of sensitivity and sensibility, my selfishness and my vulnerability. The burden of guilt was weighing heavy on my head. At that point in time, I hated everything I was addicted to. Yes, I could have saved his life, but I didn't because, a friend going through depression pretended to be rude to me, and most importantly, somewhere in my subconscious mind lurked that fatal temptation to be a part of the celebration that cost me so dearly. But forgiving him was not easy for me either. The sense of belongingness was not just a chain that could be snapped apart with so little effort. It was such an integral part of our reason to live and let our loved ones live. It was not all about "I, me and myself." It was about our togetherness, the need to share all our happiness, woes and afflictions and sail through the rough patches of life. Being together confirms and consolidates our faith in our friendship and helps us sort out our respective existential crises.

How could he take such a decision without even thinking for a while about the effects it would have on his widow mother, his brother who was still walking a few miles every day to sell fritters to the school students, pinning all his hopes on his younger brother to rescue the family from the mess? What effects would it have on both his sisters, who had reached marriageable age but were still not married because their mother and their brother couldn't afford to bear the expenses of the marriage? How could Arun so selfishly decide to leave this world when nothing was right with his family? How could he forget those vacant stares of his mother, the struggle of his brother with his destiny? How could he be oblivious of everyone, who had sacrificed at least a fraction of their happiness to build his future? How could he ever think of taking such a drastic step, while pretending all the time that, he was feeling just upset and everything would be good within a day or two or, at best, one week? Why didn't he give me a hint to let me know how broke he had been feeling all those days after what had happened between him and Ruby? I had never tried to barge into his private world. The fault was all mine for mistaking him to be a tough guy, a stable human being with unwavering self-confidence, whereas in reality, he was so weak, so fragile, so delusional. For a while, I felt a vague anger building up within myself, the anger that could neither forgive my callousness nor his betrayal. I hit the wall hard with my fist to release all my pent-up frustration but got no relief.

The local I.I.C. came after thirty minutes with his team, jostling through the crowds assembled on the corridor. The boarders were visibly agitated as most of them thought it to be a case of death due to unrequited love. The police brought down the body from the fan and completed a preliminary investigation, interrogating those who were close to him. The police also seized the suicide note that he had written on his H.S.C. Board Certificate with a disclaimer that no one was responsible for his death. Though we couldn't access the content of the note, we gathered that much information, when the IIC was briefing the media. They recorded my statement as well as the statement of his crestfallen roommate, who was crying like a child. They took his body in an ambulance for the postmortem. In the meantime, the superintendent booked a trunk call to the local post office of his village to inform his family about the tragedy. I, along with Vikash, Akash, and the Assistant Superintendent, went to the hospital to receive the body after the postmortem so that the body could be handed over to one of his cousins, who was supposed to come from Bhubaneswar.

THE DARK FACE OF THE MOON

It was an ominous night as we stood near the postmortem room of the city hospital, dimly lit by a hundred-watt electric bulb, emitting just enough light so that the cruel and complex process could be accomplished in time. An owl was hooting from the nearby banyan tree. As the doctor was busy doing the post-mortem, I was lost in my own thoughts. Death could be so ghastly! For a while, I was angry with Ruby. But Ruby had never betrayed Arun, because she had no idea that Arun could get so seriously involved with her. It was just not an ordinary case of suicide because the girl didn't reciprocate. At least, as much as I knew Arun, he could never die so stupidly. But what was the reason behind this premeditated self-slaughter? Arun was always so serious and so deeply introspective. I had never seen someone like him having such control over his emotions, someone who had always kept my rebellious spirit in check, someone who always told me not to jump to a conclusion immediately when the premises seemed unconvincing or inconclusive. How could he be the perpetrator as well as the victim of such premeditated self-annihilation? I didn't have the answer to these questions. I was standing there in a precarious condition in a dimly lit hospital corridor to receive the dead body of my friend, my solicitor, my mentor, the guy who had understood me like no one ever had, rectified my erring spirit and transformed a bohemian into a fun loving guy who could think, feel and love. The greatest irony was he became a horrible instance of self-contradiction when it was the right time for self-assertion.

When we were busy completing the formalities, I saw his cousins searching for me. Since no member of his family could reach the hospital at such short notice, the body was handed over to him after receiving a declaration form, duly signed by him. He was dithering on the dark corridor, smoking a cigarette quietly. He was a tall young man in his late twenties. He looked perceptively nervous and worried, as carrying a dead body all alone was not going to be an easy task. We could read the dilemma on his face. We volunteered to accompany him all the way to his native village, where his cremation would take place. He heaved a sigh of relief and then took a puff of a cigarette and let the smoke out to release his pent-up anxiety. Then he coughed a little to clear his throat and spoke to us, "Thanks, guys, for being so kind. I will never forget this noble gesture. It would have been very difficult for me to carry my brother's body all by myself. I came here after getting a sudden trunk call from my father. He broke the news of Arun's death to me over the phone and told me to bring his body home. Before he could complete it, the phone got disconnected. You know how difficult it is to book a lightning call from our village. But the problem for me is now to decide where to take his body, his own house or that of his uncle." I was listening to him quietly so far. But when he shared his dilemma, I lost my cool for a while. I raised my voice as I spoke; "Why to his uncle's house when he has his own home? His mother, Babu Bhai, Pari Didi and Sony Didi will be waiting for the last glimpse. Why to his Uncle's house?" I wasn't bragging about my proximity to Arun to impress his brother.

He listened to me without showing any emotion and spoke quietly. "Perhaps you guys don't know, that his uncle adopted him when his son passed away after being diagnosed with blood cancer. Arun's mother was never fond of her brother, especially after he started living separately, leaving his old and ailing father fending for himself in their dilapidated ancestral cottage. Arun's mother was coming frequently to take care of her father when he was on his deathbed. One night, the old man passed away, when there was no one to attend him. Arun's mother couldn't forgive her brother, who was blindly following his wife's diktat. But things changed after the sudden death of Arun's father. His uncle took advantage of their poverty and kept persuading his mother to allow him to take legal custody of Arun. You all know how bright Arun was as a student. How could the mother have afforded the expenses of putting him in the best educational institution? The money that he was getting from the government scholarships was irregular and few and far between. Arun was totally opposed to the idea. He stopped visiting his home even during the holidays. But when he was admitted to Ravenshaw College, he realised that it would be impossible to do without his uncle's help. Finally, he gave in. But I know, he was continuously suffering. Living in a state of self-denial is always difficult. Your Superintendent told me that, he committed suicide because he was dumped by a certain girl. But as far as I know, Arun would never do a stupid thing like that. One who has survived a Tsunami will never dread a storm. Yes, it's another thing that his failure in love might have been a trigger, but not the sole reason". His brother took a deep breath and wiped his eyes with his hanky. I was standing there, shaken to the core by the revelation. I remembered how often Arun had quoted Mark Twain: "Every man is a moon and has a dark side of him that he never wants to show to anyone". I had no idea; he was talking about himself. I pleaded to his brother with my hands folded not to tell anyone in his family about the alleged love story, because no one knew, what exactly was the cause of his death.

The Police constables kept his body on a stretcher in the ambulance, and four of us sat in two parallel rows with the dead body placed at the centre. The use of the word 'body' was so difficult to think of and almost impossible to utter. The ambulance moved slowly, carrying Arun to his final destination. At night, my tired friends were dozing off frequently as the ambulance was moving along the narrow road of the state highway through a deep, dense forest. Arun was lying on the stretcher, his body wrapped in a white cloth. I was almost in a trance, visualising Prakash Bhai lying cold and dead on the stretcher placed in front of our hostel. I wondered, whether they had become angels or ghosts and whether Arun would be able to meet Prakash Bhai at his new abode. I thought of the mysterious entity I had met near the tamarind tree. For a while, I felt a strange fear and closed my eyes. Then I cursed myself for being afraid of my friend, whom I had met today in the evening. A friend can't become a ghost. Most importantly Arun couldn't die and be a ghost to frighten his friend. He was like a phoenix. He would rise out of his ashes. I found everyone asleep except the poor driver. I asked him politely to lend me a bidi. I lighted the bidi and dragged the smoke deep into my lungs. The smoke untwirled the cluster of confusion I was grappling with inside the ambulance and gave me temporary relief. The ambulance was still running through the jungle, and the sunrise was still a few hours away........

THE SILENCE OF THE NIGHT

The jungle had its own music too, slowly reverberating with the pervasive nocturnal silence. It could be the howling of the wolf or the moaning of the jackal. It could be the buzzing of the insects or the premeditative flapping of the wings of a predatory bird. The entire jungle was singing a melancholic strain in the dead of the night, a music that someone mourning the death of his dearest friend could only feel. The forest was perhaps sharing my sorrow and paying its homage to someone who died young to leave this mundane world and choose a better dwelling place where there might not be any deception, the compulsion to tell any manipulative half-truths or live with heartbreaking lies. This could be a flight to another world, a world bereft of suffering humanity.

As we started passing through human settlements, we saw the sun rising from the east, scattering a pale orange glow on the earth. The sunlight was disgusting for someone beside whom, his friend was lying dead. I had never hated the sun so passionately until that day.

It was more like a hamlet with a few rows of mud houses, mounted with clay tiles and surrounded by a thick foliage of trees. As the ambulance drew nearer, we could hear the heart-rending wailing of his family members. The ladies were sitting on the ground and beating their heads against the walls with loud and passionate cries. The news of his death was like a bolt of lightning that had struck the little village with a catastrophic impact. For the first time, I saw his mother. She was in a state of shock, sitting in one corner, sobbing insanely for her youngest son, whom she had parted with, just to keep him alive. She was crying for someone whose death had shattered all the dreams she had been seeing for her children, a dream where the youngest saviour would be ready to lead like a general in the battle they had all been fighting against hunger and poverty. She was crying for a woman from whom the only glimmer of hope disappeared like the summer showers. She was crying for her young son who couldn't spend his childhood and adolescence with her, and when she was planning to spend the last part of her life with him, he vanished into nothingness, creating a deep, dark chasm in her heart.

I saw one old man in a white dhoti sitting on a mango tree with a queer horizontal growth, enabling the villagers to use the heavily inclined trunk as a sitting space. Perhaps he could be his Uncle because he was sitting dumb. I empathised with the man who had lost his own son when he was barely a child. Once again in his life, he had to bear the grief of losing someone, who had brought a ray of hope to his barren life. My eyes were searching desperately for Dhani Sir. But I couldn't find anyone matching the appearance, I had conjured up in my mind. In fact, I had always imagined him to be a lot like my father. Perhaps, he was not willing to believe that Arun had committed suicide. Sometimes the strongest person also runs away from the truth. I suddenly remembered my father and the pain I had caused him. I cursed myself that very moment for being so insensitive towards him.

No one was willing to believe that Arun had committed suicide. Everyone looked at us suspiciously, and rightly so. One gentleman who seemed to be educated in a village full of illiterate and gullible folks asked me, "What do the police say? Is it a clear case of suicide? Are they exploring the angle of a possibility of culpable homicide?". He looked at me with a proud smile for using the phrase before a student of one of the finest colleges in the state. I remained silent because it was the toughest question anyone had ever asked me. I knew and yet didn't know the answer. I stood there like a criminal, ready to plead guilty for a crime I had not committed. Nothing feels heavier than bearing the burden of an untold truth.

It was finally decided to start the funeral march from the place where he was born. They carried his body amidst soulful wailing and chanting of the one and ultimate truth in life: "The only truth in life is God. Hail to the holy spirit: *Ram naam satya hai, Hari naam Satya hai*". I was a part of the funeral procession. In a small circular patch of land surrounded by shrubs, they placed his inert body on a pile of wood and set it aflame. We left the village. I didn't have the courage to meet his mother or brother to give them some false consolations. In fact, I had nothing to share with the bereaved family except my grief, which seemed so shallow compared to theirs. There, on the outskirts of the village, the funeral pyre burnt the last remains of a person I loved so deeply.

I left the village with a sense of loss that was irretrievable. The fact that Arun was a helpless victim of circumstances, that neither let him live nor die might not sound too convincing an explanation to most of us. The very next day Saswati came to meet me. Far from being happy in her company, I felt unreasonably irritated. I wanted to be left alone. I wanted to go back home and meet my parents. I wanted to tell them that, I would never ever leave them alone in this life. I wanted to detoxify myself by releasing all the repressed negativity that stood like a wall between me and my father. I wished to be resurrected once again. I couldn't talk to Saswati for more than five minutes. She stood there in silence, waiting for me to speak, but I didn't have a word to utter. My grief became so personal that day that, I was not ready to share it with anyone. I acted in a strange manner that frightened her. She said goodbye to me and slowly walked away. That was the last time I had met her. She walked away from my life forever. She never forgave me, and I still do not know what went wrong with me that day.

THE MAZE

We got access to his suicide note. It was short and simple but profoundly disturbing. "I hold no one responsible for my death. I hold no grudge, no ill feelings, no anger, no hatred against anybody. I want to die, because I don't want to live like a corpse on a lofty throne after losing the biggest battle of my life. I don't know why and how I am slowly suffering from a delusional psychosis and I know I won't be normal again. I leave you all with one regret in life: I have disappointed all those who have loved me deeply and trusted me more than they trust themselves. Forgive me if you can"

Was he really a victim of delusional psychosis? Why so? He was always so emotionally stable. We used to look forward to drawing strength and emotional support from him during a period of crisis. What was it that pulled him to the whirlpool of emotional turbulence? I was lost in a maze, looking for a way out, which I never found. I tried hard to give myself the benefit of the doubt of not being guilty of saving his life on that fateful day. There were so many loose ends of the reel of thread, which I struggled to untangle, albeit unsuccessfully. Just two days after his death, I went back home, depressed, dejected, forlorn and lost, carrying the baggage of my guilt and failure. I left my hostel with a lingering look on the parapet, where we used to sit together for hours, and I left the place which was so dear to me with regrets galore and with a stern vow to quit that campus and never come back to that cursed place ever again in my life, the last act of cruelty I decided to inflict upon myself. I didn't know who had betrayed Arun. But all I knew was that, I had betrayed myself that day.

When I was at home after Arun's death, I was hounded by a sense of guilt that kept growing within me as a poisonous weed. The nights were disturbed by terrible nightmares, and the days were more difficult to spend. My parents were worried for me. They were certainly not prepared to see their only son in a state of deep despair. Even though I was not responsible for Arun's death, yet I lived with the regret of not being able to unravel the unsaid story of the darkest part of his life. I certainly had a chance to save his life, but I failed.

When my results came out, I had enough reasons to be happy, because once again I got, what I didn't deserve. It was no surprise to me when I learned that Arun's performance was abysmally low, considering his academic achievements in the past. It was inevitable. My parents were disappointed to see me sleeping in my room and crying with my head pressed on the pillow. I wanted to spill all the tears I had held back for over a month. I wanted a deluge of tears to inundate me and take me away to another world, where Arun would be reduced to just a memory. It took me years to start a normal life.

One week after the publication of the result, I went to the college to receive my grade sheet and transfer certificate since I had decided to quit the campus of my dream for good. When I was standing in a queue in front of the fee collection counter, I noticed Ruby in a parallel row meant for the girls. I turned my face away in my attempt to ignore her. I was certainly not ready to see Ruby so soon when I was mourning Arun's death. I stood in the queue, waiting impatiently for my turn to come to deposit my fees and get the clearance to take the documents. Each second got longer than a year, and I felt a strong, uneasy sensation in my stomach. For a while, I thought I would throw up.

After depositing the bank receipt, I heard a feminine voice calling me by my name when I was heading towards my department. I knew it was Ruby's. There was a desperation in her voice that I loathed to hear. I quickened my pace to avoid her. But she ran all the way to catch up with me. "Rajiv", She said, "Please listen to me, at least once. I won't say anything in self-defence, I have lost that right, and even if I speak, nobody would ever trust me. I have not slept for one night in all these days. It's a terrible feeling of guilt that I can not get rid of. I can't live, I can't die, I can't undo what others think I have done, I can't prove my innocence. I am damned forever. Rajiv, please listen to me for a second, and you don't have to believe me. I admit, my mistake was trying to get close to Arun. But that is something so common in our society. I should have thought about Arun and how he would be taking this relationship, and that was my fault. I was so insensible, thoughtless, whimsical. It was a sin Rajiv, and I deserve to be punished. But the fact is, I was never in love with him. Trust me, I was……" I cut her short, "That's enough, Ruby; I am not at all keen to hear your part of the story. Every line you speak today leaves me angry and devastated. In fact, if one person is guilty, then it's me. I have to live with it throughout my life. Please go away and live your own life. I don't know if I will ever get a chance to meet you, and I sincerely pray that never happens. Goodbye." With one last look, I left the place. Ruby was standing there with her head hung. I couldn't say whether she was crying that day. But she was in pieces after the storm.

EPILOGUE

THE ROAD TO REDEMPTION

(i)

In the meantime, thirty years have elapsed, and for years together, I have tried to contemplate a logical completion to the story that remained buried deep within my heart under the sediments of memories, sad and disturbing, which can never be swept away by the currents of a dark, deep river called oblivion. While struggling with the blues commonly associated with what metaphorically one calls the afternoon of one's life, I have never missed one quiet night to put things together to end my story somewhere in a space where darkness meets light, dreams are etched against reality and visions are mixed with voices I had seen and heard, partly forgotten and partly remembered. Reality needs no garb. After thirty years, I recall a few old familiar faces that were once an inseparable part of my life. I recall the painful memory of bidding farewell to a friend who died young, leaving me all alone to explore the life, that was so listless during the initial few years after his death. I recall the last moment of misunderstanding with the girl who had never forsaken me, no matter how rude I was to her. I remember the guys who had once made this life worth living when I was about to crumble down under the pressure of repressive parental pressure. I miss all those beautiful days. But one can't cling to the past for an indefinite period. It is the pastness of the past, that intervenes with our present, making it difficult to accept the eternal flux of time as the only reality. However, life moves on.......

After I left the campus, I did my post-grad at the university of my choice. I didn't have the patience to wait too long for a job in my home state when the country was passing through an unprecedented economic recession. Luckily, I didn't have to try very hard to get a job as a college teacher with a reasonably decent salary in one of the northeastern states, where I spent six beautiful years of my life in a small city with some truly wonderful people before I came back to my home state with a stable job. In the meantime, I was lucky enough to get married to a girl who shouldered all my cares and anxieties without any grudges or grumbles. Responsibilities kept piling up with time, slowly but steadily alienating me from my past. My contact with my friends became less frequent. It's not that I forgot them, but my primary responsibility was taking care of my priorities, which kept changing with time. Honestly speaking, being a son, a husband and a father became more important than being a friend. I told you in the beginning it's all about being and becoming.

Nowadays, I meet a few of my friends occasionally, who were very close to me once. I meet them in occasional reunions. But we never recall that ghastly night. I lost touch with Saswati the day we parted with a bit of unpleasantness. One of my friends once told me that she had married a Delhi-based doctor. I shouldn't have been so harsh to her that day. One has to pay a price for ruining a beautiful relationship with unprovoked harshness. I was certainly not in the right frame of mind, and the reason was not very hard to explain to everyone else, except Saswati. She had never forgiven me after that incident. Had I not been there at Arun's funeral procession, I would have been in a better state of mind while reciprocating Saswati's sympathy, which had always been so genuine. Moreover, it was my sense of guilt that took possession of me like a demon that day. But that never justifies my insensitive behaviour towards her.

I still see Arun in my dreams, the young Arun who had spent his adolescence with me for years in two different hostels. I sometimes see him sitting near my bedside, looking anxiously into my face. I feel his ethereal presence in my living room as if, he has been staying with me in a formless form. But I have stopped visualising that horrifying sight of seeing him hanging from the ceiling fan.

Life has been a topsy-turvy journey for me along a meandering path that leads nowhere. I still miss those good old hostel days. At every reunion, we all have that feeling of Deja-vu. While gulping and guzzling in the hotel, we forget that, we are standing at the threshold of old age and behave like crazy teenagers. I was not a good son and could not be a good husband, but I have always tried to remain humane throughout my life.

It was the 23rd of May. I was home, enjoying the third quarter of the much-awaited summer vacation. There was nothing much to do except complete a few pending academic assignments. My son had come home on a week-long sabbatical from his workplace to spend a few days with us. On the 22nd night, I told my wife and my son that, we would be going on a trip to the countryside the next day. It would be a six-hour journey from our home town, so it was likely to be a bit tiresome. I asked them to pack the essentials so that, we could start early. My son was not very enthusiastic, and my wife was surprised to see me withholding details of the destination we would visit the day after. She wanted to elicit the truth from me, but I was tight-lipped. Nobody was happy with me. So, the question of sharing my enthusiasm was a foregone conclusion. I told them that it would be an adventure, but neither of them was adventurous.

We woke up early in the morning. At around 5.30 AM, we hit the highway with my son in the pilot seat. The sky looked golden with the mellow light of the rising sun. After covering a distance of 75 kilometres, we took a diversion to the right. The remaining sixty kilometres would be through a state highway. I had been to this part of the state only once while carrying the mortal remains of Arun to his village, though I had spent a large part of my life serving in the hinterland as a government servant. A lot has changed in these thirty years. We were no longer travelling through the meandering paths of a jungle. The road had been broadened enough to make driving a pleasant exercise. We stopped near roadside dhabas and tea stalls at regular intervals to make the journey less tedious. When I was interacting with the shop owners, my son looked at me curiously, because he had never seen his father getting so hyper on any road trip we had undertaken together. We travelled through the grey and bare patches which were once deep, dense forests. I found no stream, no stiff mountain climbing. There were human settlements everywhere. Small bazaars had cropped up here and there, and shops were dealing with essentials. The topography had radically changed over the years. As my son was navigating our car through this unknown patch of land, my eyes were fixed on the GPS tracker on the dashboard. Thirty years is a fairly long time to obliterate my memory of the landscape I had visited only once. That night, I was not in the right frame of mind after being unsettled by the burden of grief and the final feeling of not being trustworthy enough after I heard the shocking revelation from Arun's cousin.

It was around noon when we reached our destination, Arun's native village. The sun was blazing down on the newly laid village road. I had not forgotten his father's name. After making a few queries to some of the local people, I was able to come very close to his ancestral home. I decided not to visit any of his family members because I didn't want to scratch an old wound. My son was perceptibly perplexed, and so was my wife. But my wife, who had heard Arun's story earlier, had formed a vague idea about the purpose of the visit based on her intuition. From a distance, I saw a concrete house standing in the place of the old mud house. One of the villagers told me that, the family was much better off financially. Babu Bhai has expanded his business, which is now managed by his sons. Arun's mother died a couple of years ago. God had been kind enough to keep her alive long enough to see her son doing well. The man was all praise for Babu Bhai and the way he had handled the responsibilities of the family after Arun's death. I was relieved to hear that, Arun's sisters were all happily married. I got down from the vehicle and walked towards the crematorium where the last rites of Arun were performed. I stood there for a while trying to find a memorial for Arun, and I was not very surprised to find none. By the way, who remembers someone who had run away from life? While returning, I saw a small signboard on a building almost in ruins on the outskirts of his village. The weather-beaten signboard has withstood the ravages of time. Amidst a few fading letters, all I could read was the word "Ashraya". It was perhaps the same shelter home, where Arun had spent the most painful period of his childhood.

The entire experience was purgatorial. When we were coming back, my son asked me, "Why did you come to this place? Why did you come back without meeting anyone? What was the purpose of this strenuous, long journey"? I could sense the disappointment and a trace of anger in his voice. As I manoeuvred the steering while negotiating a bend, I told him, "Have patience. Today, your Papa will tell you the story of that part of his life, he has never shared with you".

(ii)

A few days after I visited Arun's birthplace, one evening, while sitting in a bar cum restaurant, where people with a distinct taste for good food and drinks hang around, I saw a lady sitting on a table opposite me with a glass of red wine. She must be of my age. She looked so elegant and strangely familiar. I saw the lady looking curiously at me. To my surprise, she stood up and slowly came towards me. "Ain't you Rajiv from English Honours at Ravenshaw College?" she asked. There was a familiar ring in her voice. "Oh yes, You are, I can't be wrong. Hey, don't you recognise me? I am Saswati. I looked at her in surprise. The intimacy in her voice, even after thirty long years, had not worn out a bit. I felt like standing up and giving her a warm hug. But I had to restrain myself because the glass ceiling was still not broken. I still carry the remorse of hurting her for no apparent reason, when she came running all the way from her home to console me. "Hey, how could you recognise me so easily, when I look like a ghost of my former self?" I asked her in disbelief. She still looked sweet, though she had put on a bit of weight with age.

I moved to her table. While she was sipping her red wine, I took two large pegs of Vodka. The urge to go back to our past that we had lost, while traversing a long distance in life, was so overwhelming. I could read a chastened sadness on her face. Discovering Saswati so unexpectedly in a place that I love to visit so frequently seemed so incredibly exciting. I had all the time in the world to spend with her that night to make amends for the mistake I had made thirty years ago.

Life had never been kind to her. She got married to a doctor at the age of twenty-two when most of her friends were at the university. Her father was diagnosed with pancreatic cancer, and to make the dying man happy, Saswati married a person she didn't know. After the honeymoon, she shifted to Delhi. During the first few days, her husband pampered her with all his love and care. But later on, things started falling apart. He started coming back home late, giving one excuse or another and the number of excuses kept multiplying every day. Saswati had to believe all those cock and bull stories he cooked up every night, which he could narrate so convincingly to his unsuspecting wife. One fine evening, at a family party, she saw a lady whom her husband introduced to her as one of his colleagues. But later, she came to know from a nurse from the same hospital that Saswati's husband was having an affair with her. Before his marriage, he was in a sort of live-in relationship with her. But he had to marry Saswati due to family pressure as Saswati's father was a childhood friend of the father of Dr Deepak, Saswati's husband.

When Saswati confronted her husband, he confessed, because he knew it would happen one day. He wasn't even apologetic about cheating on his wife. Saswati pleaded with him and begged him to come back to her life, but he was unmoved. After her father's death, she decided not to live a life full of lies and pretensions. She knew she deserved a much better life, and she didn't have to compromise with a person she didn't trust. Trust deficit is a vicious moth that can destroy a relationship. She finally decided to say goodbye to a life, that was not worth living with someone, who had so blatantly betrayed her with no feeling of guilt or remorse for not showing any accountability or commitment to the woman he was married to. She came back to her city. And now, she is working as a consultant to the NGOs, working for the rehabilitation of the poor. She said that, working for the people from whom one has no expectations, except a deep sense of gratification for being useful to somebody in life, has been such a fulfilling experience for her that, she has forgotten the pangs of betrayal, the fizzling out of dreams she had seen in her maidenhood. But she must be hiding the scar in her heart. A wound gets healed, leaving an ugly scar, a painful remembrance of the fact that, someone had hurt you once.

After dinner, we walked together on the pavement with a pleasant autumn sky overhead. Saswati suddenly said, "Do you know something very interesting? Of course, you may not like to hear this. After such a grand betrayal, I could forgive my husband. I have almost forgotten him, and strangely, I don't hold him responsible for the debacle in my life, because I was thrust on him. He didn't marry me out of his own choice. Perhaps it was predestined, a part of God's larger plan. But I have never been able to forgive you, Rajiv, for the way you had hurt me that day. You know, that was the first and the last occasion I had lied to my father and slipped out of my house to be with you. I will never forget that rude behaviour, that killing indifference in your eyes. For a while, I thought you were holding me responsible for Arun's death. I cried all the way in the autorickshaw and promised myself never to meet you again". I listened to her in silence. I am always more of a punching bag, so bad at self-defence. I was still consumed by that guilt. I was certain I would never be able to convince her what went wrong with me that day.

She again broke the silence when I was lost in my thoughts, "I am sure you don't know, but I still want to tell you today that, I was always in love with you, even though I still wonder why. You were so mediocre in every respect. But I was persistently and hopelessly in love with that mediocre boy in my class. I could not gather the courage to tell you my feelings for you, because you had never been serious about anything in life. I told you today because, at this age, what happened in the past would hardly matter to you, and even if it did, you can't simply dump your wife and fall in love with me. And if you dare do that, I will neither forgive you nor give you back the place, that I had once given you. No one knows it better than me, Rajiv, how it feels when you realise that you have been betrayed by someone with whom, you have spent a portion of your life, at least with some kind of trust. It doesn't matter how significant or insignificant that portion may be. No one wants to be betrayed. Why did I tell you today that, I was in love with you, even though it has now become the old yellow pages of the history book of our college days? I would love to see your reaction after hearing something you had never dreamt of hearing ever in your life from someone like me. This was the score I was waiting to settle with you all these years, though the hope of meeting again was so flimsy. Honestly, I wonder how often you might have deceived your wife by telling her you love her. But the truth is you have never loved anyone with the same passion or the same intensity as you have loved yourself, and the damn bloody truth is, you are not capable of having the feeling of being in love with someone. You are a narcissist who is obsessed with his love for himself. At least you were. Do you remember the story I told you about Echo and Narcissus? Like Echo, I just imposed my goddamn presence on you while you were looking at your own reflection and falling in love with it, and I could not bring you out of that trance. But unlike Echo, I left you where you were, stuck in your private world with your hopeless predilection. I didn't curse you like Echo but distanced myself from your world to see you experimenting with the objective detachment you were so proud of during our college days, which I always perceived as disguised self-love".

There was some bitterness in her statement. But wasn't she right? Maybe my love for my freedom was an obsessive personality disorder. That could be the reason why Arun distanced himself from me a few days before his death. Saswati's confession didn't hurt me. Rather, it had a healing effect on me. At least I got to know, what I had done and undone in my past.

I got the answer to the question, that had been haunting me for the last thirty years. There is no better feeling than to be loved and lost, and there is no worse feeling than being afraid of falling in love. I could only mumble a lame 'Sorry' to Saswati as she was going to her car. When she was about to leave, I stopped her and continued, "Saswati, you have always come to my rescue whenever I found myself in a tight spot. Today, I am asking you to do me another favour; hopefully, the last instalment". She stopped on her way, with a little apprehension may be. I told her about my visit to Arun's village. I added, "I saw the orphanage, 'Ashray', where Arun had spent his painful childhood. I wanted to do something for those underprivileged children and was wondering what and how to do it. Together, let's try to save at least some of them". She smiled with a glint in her eyes. This time, she knew what I expected of her, and I knew she would never disappoint me. I asked her to call me whenever she felt lonely or depressed and that she could count on me. I knew how shallow that sounded, especially when it came from someone like me with a checkered history as a friend. She just gave a sly nod. Was it of denial or acceptance? Only time will say.

I have lost one friend due to that irredeemable self-obsession. I don't want to lose another friend again. As I looked up, I saw shades of colours forming a luminous arc that resembled a rainbow in the sky. Each shade of colour reflected a tapestry intertwined with an intricate pattern of emotions. I stood on the pavement with my eyes fixed on Saswati's car. When she was telling me the story of Echo and Narcissus, I recalled the curse of Devyani, the curse with which Kaccha lived his life without letting Devyani know his part of the story, and there was never hope for redemption for Kaccha. Kaccha knew it was not going to end so soon…It was just the beginning that knew no end.

It's time for me to look for a shooting star in the sky and make a wish. It is time for me to remember a wish

I had made long ago on seeing a shooting star in the midnight sky. It is time for me to be myself.......

THE DARK RAINBOW

Who knows you better than a poet

The one who battles it out every day

His patience never gives in

His resilience you find so seductive

As you fiddle with his pain

He never lets you know

Where it hurts the most

His privacy is so dear to him

You keep hammering on his head

Drill holes in his heart

He doesn't cry, he doesn't protest

He writes one more song for you

You are still his unrequited love

The climax of his untold story

The crescendo in his unheard musical note

You crush him like a reptile

Look curiously to see the pain in his eyes

You feel the triumph when he is ripped apart

He smiles at you

He clings to you

You are his pain

You are his sorrow

The dark rainbow in his purple sky

But hold on!

You are and you will always be

His only pretext to live, love and ideate.

The End

www.ingramcontent.com/pod-product-compliance
Lightning Source LLC
La Vergne TN
LVHW091303150826
845673LV00006B/1517

* 9 7 9 8 8 9 5 5 6 9 6 8 9 *